TAKEN BY THE ORC

MINA CARTER

Join my VIP reader list and be the first to hear the news on book releases, AND be eligible for subscribers only bonus content, giveaways, special offers and free reads!

Don't miss out, sign up now!

SIGN UP HERE

ABOUT TAKEN BY THE ORC

She's always loved fairy tales. Starring in one isn't on her bucket list...

Not that Hope has much of a bucket list, except in her head. Forced to work for a pittance by her cruel stepfather, she has no way out of the drudgery of her life. Being mugged in the park at night is just par for the course... until a big, green monster rescues her.

Rather than waking up in a hospital bed with a severe concussion as she expects, she's whisked off to a fantastical land filled with all the creatures from her childhood stories. Only she quickly realizes that not everything beautiful is nice, and her big, green monster is not what she expected. A battle-scarred warrior, he might be her only chance of getting home alive.

And, well... it doesn't hurt that he's put together like a Greek god, but boasting about his... equipment doesn't get him on her good list. Saving her from certain death though... yeah, that might do it.

Between a witch's curse and a treacherous court, Hope must make a choice about her future and whether her monster lives or dies...

CHAPTER ONE

"Oh, for God's sake, useless girl, stop daydreaming about a fairy-tale prince sweeping you off your feet. These tables won't clean themselves. Will they?"

Hope Howell jumped at the sharp sound of her stepfather's voice, banging her head on the underside of the table. For a moment she closed her eyes at the taunt that had followed her since she was twelve and had once sighed at the scene in a fairy-tale movie where the prince had swept the heroine off her feet and carried her off so they could live happily ever after.

She sighed. What she'd give for a prince to ride by and sweep her off her feet... but it wasn't going to happen. One, princes were in short supply these days and two, shit like that only happened in fairytales, not in the life of one, down-on-her-luck orphan called Hope Howell.

With a grimace, she scraped the last of a sticky mess of gum from underneath the table, dropping it into the waste bucket she held. She would never understand what drove people to stick the stuff there, when trash cans sat literally less than two steps away. But then, people usually defaulted to easy rather than doing what was right.

"No, of course not, Mr. Hanbury," she murmured, quickly emerging from under the table. She rubbed the lump on the back of her head circumspectly as she avoided her stepfather's laser-like gaze. She knew better than to argue or call him stepfather. Harold Hanbury didn't accept "excuses," especially not from her, and he absolutely didn't want anyone to know they were related, albeit by marriage. "I'll get on that right away."

"You'd better," he grumbled in a low voice as she swept a quick, worried glance around the cafe. But it was as clean as a whistle. The only table that needed clearing was over by the door, where the café's last customers of the morning had just headed out.

She grabbed her cleaning rags and headed that way. If they got clear of the door and she wasn't already clearing the table, her stepfather would find a whole list of new chores that had to be done before she left tonight.

Hanbury's Hot Bites was a hot spot in the local area, their pastries and delicacies raved about in all the foodie magazines. Harold had held court at each and every interview, a wide smile on his face as he stood for the camera with his arms looped over the shoulders of her stepbrothers, Jacob and Isaac. "Local Family Makes Good," the headlines read, each reporter gushing about the handsome owner, a silver fox no less, and his two equally handsome sons.

She scrubbed at the table, making sure no marks or stains at all were left on the surface. The words left her cold. What none of the interviews or reports said was that Hanbury's Hot Bites used to be Howell's Tea Rooms... her mother's pride and joy. Now no one remembered her or realized Hope was up at the ass-crack of dawn baking. Instead, Harold and his asshole sons took all the credit.

But it seemed even her rapid response was not enough to put the three Hanbury men off.

"She's too busy daydreaming about a prince coming to take her away," Jacob sneered from the counter. "Not that anyone would even look twice at a dumpy plain little mouse like her."

"Yeah," Isaac chimed in from the "office," a small closet between the cafe and the kitchens. "The only way he'd come is with Pam the palm and her five little friends. No way he'd want to stick it in her."

She caught her breath, ignoring the cruel jibes. They'd been the same since her mom had died when she was eleven and she'd been left with no one in the world but Harold and his mean sons.

"Girl!" Harold barked. "When you're done, the pots need washing, and we need to prepare for tomorrow."

"Yes, Mr. Hanbury. Right away," she murmured, giving the table a last wipe-down before she headed that way and walked past him. As she was almost through, he reached out and she felt the letter pulled from her back pocket.

"What's this then?" he demanded, his eyes alight with twisted excitement and hatred as he started to unfold it.

"That's mine! Give it back!" she gasped, trying to snatch it back from him, but he laughed nastily and held it up out of her reach.

"Yours? This looks like a letter. Who said you could have mail?"

Tears filled her eyes as he finished unfolding the letter and scanned the contents. She'd applied to the local culinary college for a sponsorship program after seeing an advert on a noticeboard in a local charity shop. It came with bed and board, and she'd do anything to get away from her stepfamily.

"A sponsorship, eh? Baking?" With each word, Harold's expression got darker. "Well, we can't be having that kind of nonsense. Can we?"

"No... no, please don't," she whispered with tears in her eyes as he tore the letter into tiny pieces. A sob escaping her, she tried to grab the pieces before they hit the floor, but a hard hand clamped around her upper arm.

"Forget it, girl," Harold hissed in her face, hatred seething in his expression. "You've nowhere to go and no one wants you. Now get out there in the kitchen or you'll be going hungry tonight."

~

ears in her eyes, Hope walked to the kitchen with her head down so no one could see her expression. But once she got there, she took one look at the sink piled high with dishes and kept on walking.

She walked herself right through the kitchen and out the back door, down the alley, and caught the first bus that stopped. She ought to be thankful that Harold had been too cheap to spring for driving lessons for her and insisted she go to market on the bus because she had no money and nothing in her wallet other than her bus pass and an old library card.

Numb, she looked out of the window sightlessly as the streets passed by, absently getting off when she reached her favorite park. Her mom used to bring her here when she was a child, and she even had vague memories of coming here with her father, his large reassuring presence and vaguely accented deep voice all she remembered of him.

She clung onto those memories, and those of her mom, fiercely. They were all she had. Harold had gotten rid of everything of her mom's when she'd died, all apart from the antique chain Hope wore around her neck, carefully hidden beneath her clothes.

Walking through the main gates of the park, she took a deep breath and savored the sounds and scents of nature. This little oasis was hidden in the middle of the noise and smog of the city, yet once within its walls, the city outside didn't exist. She'd like to believe that, needing to sink into the peace and tranquility the sanctuary offered after today.

She sat on a small bench near the little play area her mother had brought her to. The slides and swings were gone now but she still heard the echoes of the past and a happier time as she sat there in the sun. Just before she'd died, her mom had told her not to worry, that Harold loved her and would look after her. Her mom would have been so furious at Harold for how things had turned out, how he'd treated her.

"I'm not going back. Not ever," she muttered to herself. Ripping up her letter was the last straw. That placement was her last and best chance of getting away from the Hanburys.

Children's laughter caught her attention and she looked up as a family stood in line for ice cream on the corner by the fountain. Longing filled her, but just like she'd had no money for a bus fare, she had no money for the treat she remembered from childhood.

In fact, all she had to her name was the small amount she'd managed to scrape together from customer tips when Harold or one of the terrible twosome didn't see it and make her hand it over. Which was most of the time.

Harold didn't even pay her for her work in the cafe, insisting that all her wages had to go toward feeding and clothing her as well as toward the rent and other bills. To hear him talk, she lived the life of a princess already with new clothes every week, rather than the hand-me-downs she wore. The shirt she had on used to be one of Jacob's while the jeans were from a charity shop close to the cafe. Her only extravagance were her boots, found brand new at the same charity shop. She'd worn them for years and they were still going strong.

She didn't know how long she sat there wrapped in her own memories, but eventually the shadows lengthened, and it began to get cold. So cold that mist had started to roll in, gathering in the growing shadows around the bushes and under the trees. Shivering, she pulled her thin jacket closer. Her adamant declarations to herself that she wasn't going back wavered as it got colder. At least the former store room at the back of the cafe that Harold let her "rent" was warm. And she was hungry too. All there was to eat would be leftovers and what hadn't sold in the cafe, but at least it was food that would fill her belly. Besides, if she was going to leave, she at least needed her things. They'd all fit in a small pack, but... yeah, she stopped thinking along those lines. It was depressing to think all she owned in the world would fit in a small bag.

Shoving her hands deep in her pockets, she stood and walked out of the park. They'd be closing the gates soon anyway and she didn't want to get locked in. Not that she couldn't get out. There was... or at least used to be... a small gap in the fence behind the pavilion she could squeeze through. But she felt so battered and heart-sore that she couldn't be clambering around and grubbing in the dirt.

Heading to the bus stop, she checked the timetable and sighed. The last bus was ten minutes ago.

"At least the walk will keep me warm," she muttered to herself and turned toward "home."

After a few minutes of walking, the hackles on the back of her neck rose. She was being followed.

"*Shit.*" Her shoulders stiffened and slowly, so as not to alert her follower that she was onto him, she sped up. Luckily, she knew this area like the back of her hand, so it was nothing to speed up, duck down an alley and run like freaking hell.

Her heart pounded, her boots splashing through puddles as she raced down one alley, turned left, right, and then right again. Her breath rasping in her ears almost deafening her, she tucked herself into an old, boarded-up doorway and crouched down to peer around the battered, brick edge.

Why would someone be following her? It wasn't like she was pretty or anything, certainly not the type who got attention from men. Hell, she could walk past a site full of builders without a single catcall. And her clothing screamed out the fact she didn't have any money... so why would someone possibly want to follow her?

Keeping her breathing as light as possible, she watched the alleyway. At the first sight of movement, she flipped the hood on her dark jacket up and folded her hands out of sight. With each slow breath in and out she concentrated on being invisible. This trick sometimes worked when she didn't want to be seen, so she hoped and prayed it worked now.

Heavy footsteps passed by in front of her, splashing in one of the puddles left over from last night's rain. Whoever it was, they were *heavy*. Which meant big. Which meant she definitely didn't want to come face to face with them. Holding her breath, she waited until the steps reached the end of the alley and turned.

Then she ran, darting out from her hiding place and going back the way she'd come.

She made it to the first turn, rounding the corner before slamming into someone. Someone large, round, and smelling of cheap liquor. She rebounded from him as hard hands grabbed at her upper arms for a moment before they went down in a tangle of limbs.

She heard a crash of breaking glass and she winced as she hit the ground hard.

"Look at what you made me do, girl!" a harsh voice snarled, and she found herself pinned down with bleary, bloodshot eyes glaring down into hers. "You're gonna have to give me something for that!"

CHAPTER TWO

"Oh, come on, Buttercup... No one will know. It's just a small cuddle. What's it going to hurt?"

Graal lay back on the sumptuous bed in his tent and watched the whore dress quickly. She was a pretty little thing, a half orc like all of them, but what her other half was he didn't know. Whenever he'd asked, she'd refused to tell him, tossing her straw-blonde hair and telling him to guess. His guess would have been fae, and he knew that was why she was so popular. A lot of orcs, him included, fantasized about pinning down a lovely faery and fucking the breath out of her... not that any of them would ever admit to it, of course. Orcs and fae had been enemies for centuries. No orc would ever find a fae attractive, or sexy. No way, no how.

So Buttercup (definitely not her real name) and the other whores who looked even vaguely fae-like did a roaring trade in the orc camps.

"You know the rules, handsome. No cuddling, no

"

kissing... not even for up the ass. That costs extra." She looked over her shoulder as she laced her corset up. Only halfway, mind, the better to show off the obscenely large tits she had for such a small frame. "Now, where's me money?"

She leaned forward and readjusted her corset so the very edges of her nipples peeked over the top. Graal cupped his cock half-heartedly and she eyed him speculatively.

"Is that an invitation? Because if not, I've gotta ride Thorlack's cock this morning. But I could do that after breakfast if yours is on offer."

The very mention of her other clients deflated Graal's cock completely. He didn't want sex. He wanted a warm, curvy form pressed up against his for a lazy morning in bed.

"Coppers are on the side," he grunted, rolling out of bed and reaching for some breeches.

Unlike most of the orc army, he preferred to wear dress clothes, his trunks filled with fine clothing he'd had made by local seamstresses in the towns and villages the army passed. But even the mention of wearing a shirt around here and the barbarians scoffed and made fun of him. He beat the shit out of most of them if they didn't run away fast enough, which meant he'd just get blood on his nice shirts anyway, so he didn't bother. Breeches and some boots were as far as he went.

"Got 'em!" the whore trilled, snatching up her payment and flouncing out of his tent. He trailed behind, watching as she waved a good morning to a trio of orcs around a nearby campfire. As she did so, she made sure her skirt flicked up, the better to show her ass—and the fact she didn't wear any underwear—off. He sighed. She knew her stuff, showing off the goods was always good for business.

"I dunno why you bother," a deep voice made him turn. Karak the Terrible, captain general of Dread King Batak's army, held out a flagon of mead in his direction.

Graal grabbed it and downed half in long swallows before sighing and wiping his mouth on the back of his arm. "What do you mean?"

"With the floozies. None of them are going to get all snuggly. No profit in it," the big general grunted as he poked bacon in a pan over the fire with his knife.

Graal's eyes narrowed at the domestic scene. Times past, Karak would either still be passed out from a dead drunk or just awake and roaring for someone to bring him more mead, and half a cow, lightly roasted, for breakfast.

His gaze flicked to the captain general's tent. Now he was cooking breakfast for his little human mate who was probably still asleep after a long night of Karak fucking her.

"Alright for you to say." He thumped down on a log next to Karak. "You probably got snuggles this morning."

"And a blow job," Karak grinned, holding out a slab of bacon to Graal on the end of his knife. "You know what the answer is. Don't you?"

He grabbed the bacon and devoured it in two bites.

His tusks, while tiny compared to Karak's, were still razor sharp. "Fuck your wife before breakfast?"

It was an automatic reply, one that got nothing more than a glower from the bigger orc. Anyone else and he'd have ripped their heads off and played football through the camp with it, but he and Graal had grown up together.

"Nope."

"What then?"

Karak rarely offered advice other than, "Stick the pointy end in the enemy," and, "Don't fucking die," so when he did, Graal listened.

"You need a human."

"That's what I've been saying. *You* have a human. We could share."

Karak lifted a thick, bushy eyebrow. "You're pretty, but I ain't fucking you."

Graal finished the rest of his mead in a long swallow and belched loudly. "We could both fuck her."

He'd get snuggles then. He just knew it. He'd watched Karak's mate, Kelly. She was an affectionate little thing. Pretty too. She was definitely a snuggler.

Karak's low growl warned him that was not a subject to pursue. Karak might be his friend, but that didn't mean the big, green behemoth wouldn't batter him into paste.

"...or not. How do you suggest I get a human then?" he asked, flicking his silver hair back and beginning to braid it. It was one of his few vanities, the long locks reaching almost to his waist... that and his face. Oh, and his massive cock. The ladies loved his massive cock.

Karak grunted as he piled bacon onto a plate for Kelly and nodded toward a jacket draped over the log he sat on.

"Track one."

"What? How?" Graal laughed.

Like it was that simple. Until Kelly had wandered through the mists, they'd been thought extinct in these lands.

Karak lifted his head and sniffed. "Mists are coming in."

"Mists..."

The big general looked at him like he'd grown another head and heaved himself to his feet.

"Take Claw. Track a human through the mist," he said slowly, like he was talking to a child. "Now fuck off. I've got a mate to feed and then fuck. Again."

~

Karak was the ugliest bastard alive... and also the luckiest. Graal grumbled under his breath as he heard the roar from the woods to the west of the main camp.

Fucking Karak and his "claiming chases." It was a wonder the male hadn't fucked his cock right off in the months since he'd found his little human mate. They'd certainly been at it enough.

But he was happy for his friend. At least Karak had found love... and the permanent kind, not the fleeting kind that was all Graal knew from Buttercup and her similarly named sisters. The kind that could be bought for a couple of coppers a night and belonged to another male when a new day dawned.

Which was why he was out here, looking at the mists with Claw at his side.

Even he admitted, this was the stupid plan to end all stupid plans. No one knew anything about the mists, except maybe King Batak's chief wizard, Skali. Every orc felt the dark call from the swirling ephemeral tendrils but no one in their right mind would answer. Mostly because every orc knew of someone who had wandered past the sentries and never returned.

"Okay, boy, we discussed this," he murmured, holding Kelly's old jacket out for the beast to sniff. "Let's go find me a human..."

Claw growled and then tried to eat the jacket.

"Oh, for fuck's sake," he hissed, putting a booted foot on the beast's shoulder and heaving. The fabric ripped in two loudly and he almost landed on his ass. Half the jacket and a sleeve remained in his hand as Claw threw back his head and golloped down the rest.

Lifting it to his nose, Graal sniffed. Bacon fat. That idiot Karak had dropped bacon fat on the jacket and his equally idiotic hound thought it was food.

"You're an idiot. You know that?" he told the mutated kregas hound. "I am so not helping you if it gives you the shits. Understand?"

Claw panted, drool dripping from his vicious teeth. It wasn't a good combination.

"Not a thought in that head," Graal muttered and

offered the small part of the sleeve that didn't have bacon fat on it. The hound leaned forward and sniffed.

"Got it, boy?"

Claw's tail beat the ground, his yellow eyes bright as they darted to the mists and back.

"Yeah? Okay, that's it! Let's go!"

At his words, Claw shot off like an arrow, right into the swirling mists. With a deep breath and a prayer to any deity stupid enough to listen to an insane half-orc, Graal plunged into the mists after him.

They were cold.

And wet.

Which was totally expected of mist. He'd suffered through many a misty morning during campaigns with nothing but his cloak to protect him.

What he hadn't expected was the sudden drop, nothing under his feet but air. Hands out in front of him for balance, he stumbled blindly forward and then crashed into something hard and cold.

He blinked as the mists receded and the world snapped back, finding himself looking up into a hard, impassive, and very beautiful face.

Fuck... humans were *huge!*

Belatedly he realized the hard orbs he'd grabbed onto were the human's breasts.

"Shit... that... I'm..." he stammered as he snatched his hands back, just in case the huge human decided to punt him. It was one thing to grab a female's tits when she wanted him to, or when he was paying, and quite another just to grab out of the blue. He'd learned that lesson as a very young orc—he'd been somewhat of an early starter when it came to bedsport—and knew a little courtesy went a long way in these things.

But the human didn't swing for him nor curse him and...

"Fucking idiot, Graal," he muttered to himself.

He was talking to a statue. On hindsight, the white "skin" and the lack of arms should have warned him he wasn't talking to a flesh and blood human. Oh, and the height. Kelly was tiny, not taller than him like the carved female in front of him.

Stepping back, he looked at it again. She was a fine figure of a female, perhaps one of their goddesses? He looked around quickly, realizing that wherever the mists had deposited him, night was beginning to fall.

Which was perfect. He could scout and track perfectly well in the dark. Definitely better than a human could. He'd heard Kelly blundering around blindly at night and heard Karak's story's over and over again at how easy it was to track and claim her in the dark.

"Claw! Claw! Heel boy!" he hissed as he made his way through the bushes. The mists had deposited him in some kind of park, which was good news. If humans frequented this place, he could find a female, grab her, and be back before lunch.

Movement in the undergrowth warned him a moment before the battle hound slunk out from cover, the odd fluffy grass here catching on the ruff of fur down the middle of his scaled back.

Giving a hand signal for silence, he pushed forward through the bushes, only to freeze as he realized a human female stood right there in front of him. At least, he thought it was a female. Her hair was caught up under some kind of cap and the clothes she wore were shapeless, so it was difficult to tell.

Lifting his head, he breathed in experimentally and then grinned. Oh, yes, that was definitely a female, and she smelled *so* fucking good.

He held his position as she pushed off from the bench, standing to walk away from him through the park. Sliding out from the shadows, he followed her.

Luck was with him. She was human, and female, and his for the taking.

CHAPTER THREE

Hope screamed and squeezed her eyes tightly shut as the drunk's fist slammed down toward her face. She tried to bring her hands up to protect herself. Her screams rattled her skull, rebounding off the brick walls of the alley to deafen her.

The blow she was expecting didn't materialize and she realized the screams were too loud and too deep. Cracking an eyelid, she found herself in the middle of a scene from a horror film.

Her attacker was being held in the air by his throat, his feet dangling at least a foot off the ground, by a monster. Big and green with silver hair, he snarled as he shook the drunk from side to side like a dog with its favorite chew toy. Since her attacker must be well over six feet and somewhere north of two hundred and fifty pounds, this was an impressive feat of strength. The drunk's face was purple, his eyes wide with fear, and she didn't blame him. From the massive teeth, right down to the clawed feet, she'd never seen anything so... so... monstrous.

She screamed again, and he whirled around, his glowing eyes focusing on her. They swept her and then narrowed in fury before he rounded on his victim again.

Then he spoke, his voice like a rockslide. "You fucking asshole, attacking a defenseless female like that. You're at least three times her size! What's it feel like to be picked on by someone bigger than you, huh?"

He punctuated each word with another shake, his accent strangely familiar, but she couldn't place it.

"We don't like bullies where I'm from. You know what we do to them?" he snarled right in his victim's face.

The drunk shook his head, his mouth moving soundlessly, like a guppy.

"We break every bone in their body," the monster's voice deepened in threat. "Then we bunch them all together and... shove them right up their own ass."

She blinked, managing to scoot backward until her back hit the wall. As a threat, that was impressive—the drunk going white—but she was fairly sure it was physically impossible. What also seemed impossible was the sly sideways look the big green monster slid her.

Right before he winked.

Her fear receded. Monsters did not wink. Therefore she must be dreaming. She'd read a book once on dreams and their meanings. So what deep, dark part of her psyche had conjured up a giant with dental work like a warthog?

"Don't you dare," he warned the purple-faced man in his clawed grip. "Don't you fucking d—"

The acrid stink of urine filled the alley and the monster dropped the drunk, pushing him away. The guy stumbled as his feet hit the ground but picked up speed, racing away down the alleyway, falling and stumbling as he went.

"Fucking coward," the monster grumbled, dusting his hands off before he turned toward her.

She found herself unable to breathe as his bright green eyes fixed on her. They weren't emerald green. They weren't even a *nice* green but somewhere between yellow and bile green, the kind of green used in zombie horror films right before someone got their face bitten off.

Then he smiled and showed off teeth like butcher's knives. "Hi, pretty female."

The fear slammed into her again. She screamed, scrambled to her feet, and ran.

"Seriously?" he roared behind her, his huge feet pounding like jackhammers against the broken pavement and concrete of the alley as he came after her. "I was being nice and everything!"

She didn't care. She just ran, harder and faster than she ever had before as she sped through the back alleys, twisting and turning in an effort to throw the monster off her trail. But in her panic, she took a left instead of a right at a critical junction.

"*Shitshitshit...* no," she breathed as she came to a stop in a blind alley.

Spinning around, she watched as the monster

appeared at the turn, filling the gap between the buildings. His shoulders practically brushed the battered brick. Mist swirled around him. Mist that looked wrong, slick and oily... dark like the mists that swirled in her nightmares. The ones that stole her father away.

"I'm dreaming," she decided, backing away until her back hit the wall behind her. Heavy footsteps approached, and she screwed her eyes tightly shut. "Okay, I passed out on the bench. I haven't been eating right..."

Harold had sold the cafe's leftovers to a pig farm to "cover costs" due to keeping her, which meant she'd had less to eat recently.

"I've lost weight..." she whispered, feeling the monster's cool breath on her face. She scrunched her nose up, expecting it to stink. But it didn't. Instead, it—

"Minty fresh?"

Her eyes snapped open and she found him right there in front of her. So close she could feel the heat of his body beating at hers even through her clothes.

He offered a small smile as he looked her over.

"Hard to tell in those shapeless clothes, but you do look very small and scrawny. Not a problem, though. I am a good hunter and a better warrior. I will feed you up until you are healthy and curvy enough to carry my child."

"What?" She blinked. "Who said anything about kids? I don't want any monster kids!"

He grunted, his gaze assessing as he looked down at her. Fuck, he had to be well over six feet.

"Would it help if I said I had a big cock?"

Her eyes about bugged out of her head. "What? No! Why would that help?"

He looked disappointed and then shrugged. "Dunno. That usually seems to persuade females."

"Well, not *this* female... errr, woman!"

The mist had reached them now and she shuffled backward as it coiled around her ankles.

"You could ride it if you like?" he offered, the mists coiling up behind him in the shadows of the alley.

"No! Why would I want to do that?"

Seriously, her nightmares were the weirdest. Even she couldn't believe that she stood here, arguing about riding monster cock with the owner of said monster cock.

His eyebrows waggled. "So you can make your mind up about its impressive length and girth. Many have."

She arched her eyebrow. Was that supposed to convince her?

"Tempting, but I'll pass, Monster. Thanks all the same."

~

Graal hadn't managed to talk to Karak's little human mate Kelly as much as he'd have liked. Mostly because the big, ugly asshole was usually screwing her, and that kind of thing tended to distract a female from conversation. But he'd enjoyed the conversations he'd managed to get with her, finding the human intelligent with a keen wit.

So he was delighted to find the same light of intelligence in the eyes of the little female in front of him.

"You jest," he decided, grinning in delight. She must be. No female had ever passed up a ride on his massive cock with a straight face like that before. A good sense of humor boded well for her intelligence and their future together. He liked to laugh and joke as much as the next orc.

He studied her with a smile. She was kind of small and scrawny but, now he could see her face more clearly, she was passably pretty. Her hair was a dark mass of curls around her head, her dark eyes sharp and perceptive as she looked at him, and her lips were pleasantly curved. He would certainly be happy to see them wrapped around his cock, hopefully in the near future. Perhaps as she thanked him for removing her from what appeared to be a very dreary and unpleasant life.

He wanted to converse with her more. Maybe even find out her name, but the mist coiling around his ankles reminded him that he had bigger issues than the fact his little human didn't seem overly impressed with his amazing good looks nor being informed that many females had liked to ride his massive cock.

He'd been so sure that would win her over. It had with many females in the past. He looked at her more closely.

"Are you a virgin?"

"What the fuck!" she hissed, rearing back. "That's none of your business, Monster. You can't ask someone that!"

He grunted, not fooled by her outrage. Yes, definitely a virgin, which meant her reservation about his cock was understandable. She would no doubt be worried that he wouldn't be careful and would just ram his massive cock into her virgin pussy without any thought to her comfort.

A tug on his ankle reminded him that he didn't have time to debate this right now. Instead, he took a step forward and scooped her up, throwing her over a leather-armor-clad shoulder. She was so tiny compared to him that he could have fit two of her on there.

"Hey! What the hell are you doing?" she squeaked in outrage, beating tiny fists against his back. "Put me down right *now*, you... you great damn... monster!"

"Graal," he told her. "My name is Graal."

He smiled to himself as he turned and walked away down the alley, back to where the mist was at its thickest.

She'd called him a monster. That he understood. Many females called him a monster, usually in bedsport. He was very popular in the towns and villages the orc army passed, many widows and matrons wanting the fantasy of being bedded by a monstrous orc but not really ready for the reality of bedding some of the less... visually appealing of his brothers. Really, they only wished for the illusion of bedding an orc. It usually involved lots of screaming and protesting as he carried them toward their bedchambers, swiftly followed by their hands in his breeches. If they even let him wear them. Some insisted on the whole nearly naked barbarian orc scenario.

So he smiled as he used a big hand to gently swat her ass, which was surprisingly more shapely than he'd thought, as he strode toward the mists, whistling to Claw to follow on behind. The little female hadn't seen the battle hound lurking in the shadows fortunately, or she'd probably have screamed more. Even if just for effect.

The darkness enveloped them but this time he was prepared for the cold and wet. His passenger wasn't so fortunate, and he felt her gasp and then shudder.

"Fuck. Me."

Her small hiss was whispered and near to his ear. For a second his heart leaped. She'd had a change of heart and now obviously realized the advantages of bedding an orc with a massive cock as her first.

But then she shuddered violently and went from trying to get away to clinging as closely as she could. His enthusiasm dampened. Not an invite then. She was just cold. No matter, she would come around in time. Probably after she saw his impressive cock. He just had to get naked in front of her and she would fall for him.

That wouldn't be a problem. He could think of several scenarios he could set up that would require him to be naked. Swimming in the river... he could take her to a private bathhouse... hell, she didn't know anything about orcs. He could strip off, paint himself with woad, and tell her it was necessary to honor his gods before he went into battle. She wouldn't know the difference.

Satisfied he had everything if not in hand, at least plans to make his little human fall for him, he continued through the darkness. This time he was ready for the lurch that signaled the step from one world to another and landed lightly on both feet, well-balanced as he waited for the darkness and the mists to clear. He'd come through the mists slightly to the north of the orc camp, but it wouldn't take him long to get his little prize back to his tent.

The mists cleared and he looked around to orient himself—

"Fuck!" he hissed, signaling to Claw and diving for the nearest deep cover he could find, a holly bush off the main road they'd appeared on.

A main road with a mounted fae patrol headed right toward them...

CHAPTER FOUR

"Fuck? Fuck what?" Hope demanded, twisting on the big monster, Graal's, shoulders as she tried to figure out what was going on and how on earth he'd managed to get them from the alley they'd been in back to the park so quickly. "I told you before, not a chance, buddy!"

They crashed through a bush and she squeaked as the vicious barbs tore at her skin and hair. She tried to brush them away but just ended up tangled more. Graal twisted and dumped her on the cold earth, dropping down over her and shoving a big hand over her mouth.

"Keep quiet if you want to live," he murmured in a deep voice right by her ear.

She wasn't listening. Instead, she tried to wriggle free from his brutal hold, opening her mouth to sink her teeth into the fleshy part of his huge palm. But then high-pitched, tinkling laughter and hoofbeats reached her ears. She stilled, her eyes widening as she peered through the thick undergrowth to a scene right out of a high fantasy film.

Tall, beautiful people in wondrous armor rode in a group on the road in front of them. She frowned. The park didn't have any roads. It had paths but nothing wide enough to allow three horses to ride abreast like that.

In fact, she didn't recognize this area of the park at all. Logic kicked in. They must be in the back, private section that belonged to the family who had donated the park to the city.

Those thoughts were swept away as she looked more closely at the riders. They were way too tall to be human, their long hair falling down to their thighs and... they all had pointed ears.

Squeezing her eyes shut, she shook her head and reached up to rub at her eyes. When she opened them again the riders still had pointed ears.

Two more rows passed by, and they were talking in a language she couldn't understand. She tilted her head, listening. It was strange, but it felt familiar. Like she *should* understand it if she just concentrated hard enough.

She pulled at Graal's hand over her mouth, trying to ignore the rustle in the undergrowth nearby. There would be bugs... definitely bugs... probably crawling over her feet. Shuddering, she tried to ignore the sounds as Graal slowly lowered his hand, keeping it close in case she screamed or something. She looked over her shoulder, catching his gaze. He looked concerned as he watched the riders.

Her gaze dropped to his teeth. Perhaps she shouldn't have been so surprised by pointed ears when her captor had vicious tusks like that. Even so, something stopped her calling out to the riders for help.

"Fae death squad," he murmured in a voice like rocks crashing together, and he nodded to the stylized skull symbols painted on their armor as the group rode away. With a start she realized it had tusks. It was the skull of whatever Graal's people were.

"If they'd seen us, our heads would have been decorating their pikes before nightfall."

"Fae?" she breathed, not taking her eyes off the road as the last of the riders disappeared around a bend. "You mean like fairies? Fairies are *real?*"

She shifted slightly and turned to look at him, ignoring the fact her ass was damp through the denim of her jeans. The part of her that had loved fairytales and fairies as a child rushed to the fore.

"Yeah, unfortunately so," he grunted, rubbing a hand over his face before he spat on the ground. "Little winged freaks. They should all have their wings ripped off and be staked out in the sun to fucking roast."

"No!" She turned on him in horror. "Don't say that! Fairies are so cute!"

He looked at her like she'd lost her mind.

"Are you defective in the head, female? Fae are most definitely *not* cute. They're one of the most blood-thirsty and dangerous species in the realms. Stay still," he ordered gruffly. "Let me make sure it's all clear. I don't trust these fuckers not to have outriders."

She nodded, watching as he crawled forward in the

undergrowth, keeping low to the ground as he neared the edge of the road. For such a huge man... person... what even *was* he... he moved silently.

She should be running. She knew that. She should try and catch up with those riders and beg them to help her. Beg them to keep her safe from the monster right in front of her. But she didn't, staying right where she was as her father's deep voice came back to her.

Not everything that is pretty is good, pumpkin. And not everything that is ugly means you harm. Remember that.

She bit her lip and wrapped her arms around herself. She'd learned the first part of that lesson the hard way. Harold and her stepbrothers were all handsome, so handsome that women fell over themselves to date the three of them all the time. They didn't realize the Hanbury men were cruel assholes until it was way too late. She wouldn't trust any of them, nor anyone who traded on their looks, as far as she could throw them.

So she stayed where Graal had left her, watching as he lay in the undergrowth under the cover of a holly bush and looked left and right down the road.

He stayed there for so long, totally motionless, that her gaze began to wander down his huge body. His shoulders were the width of a semi at least, his waist trim even with his cloak wrapped around it, presumably to protect him from the damp undergrowth he lay on. But his ass... fuck, it was so high and tight she was sure she could bounce a handful of quarters off it.

She'd never been one to ogle a guy before, and as

soon as she realized what she was doing, she yanked her gaze away, her cheeks heating.

And looked right into a mouthful of razor-sharp teeth.

Her breathing cut out, her heart hammering, but when she opened her mouth to scream, no sound emerged other than a dry clicking. She scrambled desperately backward on her hands and ass to get away from the new threat.

It was huge, over twice the size of the biggest pit bull she'd ever seen, the mouth containing lethal teeth from ear to tufted ear. It even moved like a dog, slinking forward with predatory intent, its yellow eyes fixed on her unwaveringly. Drool dripped from its fangs to the undergrowth it crushed beneath huge, clawed paws.

"*Ohmygodpleasedon'teatme!*" she whispered, barely able to breathe as she scrabbled in the dirt and leaves for something—anything—to use as a weapon. But she found nothing, and then her back hit something solid, stopping her escape. With nowhere left to go, she kicked out, spraying dirt and stones up into the monster's face to stop it getting to her.

"Hey! Hey! Stop it!" Her big green kidnapper was there in a heartbeat, hauling her into his lap. She twisted and turned, trying to keep the monster dog in sight, only to find herself looking into the saddest, most dejected looking pair of yellow eyes she'd ever seen. The scaled dog-monster thumped its butt down in the dirt, its partially furred tail beating slowly and hopefully.

"Claw just wanted to say hi," Graal said by her ear. "He likes humans."

"What? To eat?" She twisted back to look at Graal. "Wait... that thing has a name?"

He chuckled, reaching up to tuck a loose strand of her hair behind her ear. She flinched, expecting him to cut her with his vicious claws, but instead his touch was soft and gentler than she could have imagined.

"Of course he has a name. He's a pet, not a wild animal. If he was a wild kregas you wouldn't even have seen him before he ripped your face off."

She jumped, somehow managing to limit the scream that wanted to escape down to a squeak. "That's not helping. *Really* not helping!"

Perhaps Graal realized how close to losing it she was because he motioned to the monster dog to back up. She felt guilty when it looked disappointed, side-eyeing her as Graal lifted her to her feet. He brushed her down quickly, looking determined.

"We need to get away from the road," he said, urgency filling the deep tones of his voice. "Then we need to find a place to camp until nightfall. We're deep in enemy territory, so it's not safe for us to travel during the day."

~

*H*is little female was doing a lot better than Graal had anticipated. At first he'd thought they were going to have some hysterics, especially when Claw had shoved his face in hers wanting kisses and loves. He'd thought she was going to lose it on the spot there, and Claw was still sulking that the human wouldn't cuddle him.

"What's your name, little one?" he asked as they walked, feeling a sense of hope and cautious happiness.

He'd found a human, and even though they were in fae territory, he was optimistic. They couldn't be far from the front line. Maybe a day or so of walking and they'd be home free. Then he could impress his new mate and she'd ride his cock. *Then* perhaps he could convince her to snuggle. Kelly seemed to enjoy it, so hopefully his little human would as well.

"Hope."

He almost didn't catch the word, having to turn and lean down a little when she whispered.

"You hope what, sweetheart?" He smiled encouragingly, to get her to open up a little.

"No. Hope is my name. Hope Howell."

"Hope Howl?" What an odd name for a human. "There was a famous mercenary here years ago called Howl. Any relation?"

She looked up at him and shrugged. "How would I know? I've no clue where we are."

"That... is a very good point," he conceded.

Plus, she was human. No way could a tiny, delicate little human be related to Gunther Howl, the most famous and blood-thirsty mercenary to walk the realms.

"It's a nice name. Hope," he said, testing the sound of it in his mouth. He liked it. But she didn't offer any more information, her arms folded over her chest as she kept walking beside him. He didn't mind. It was a comfortable silence. At least, he thought it was.

Which was good. He'd have had to gag her if she'd been a screamer. Even though they were in the deep woods, well away from any roads or trails, they were still in fae country. Where, though, he had no idea.

Spotting an old oak, he signaled to Hope and Claw to stay put as he climbed rapidly, swinging his weight from branch to branch to get above the tree canopy. Once he got enough height, he could look for a land-mark that might give him a clue where they were.

His expression tightened as he scanned the horizon. Nothing. Not a hill nor an outcrop of rock he recog-nized. *Shit*. The orc camp was close to the northern line, which meant he should at least see the foothills that shadowed the line or even the cursed mountains they sheltered under.

The placement of the camp was a sound strategy on King Batak's part. The fae wouldn't go anywhere near them because of the curse. No one knew what the mountains were cursed by, just that they were, and honestly, not even the orcs wanted to find out. Curses were ten a penny in the realms but antidotes and cures? Much less so. Generally the best cure for a curse was to avoid the damn thing in the first place.

But he couldn't even see the mountains, just trees as far as the eye could see. He closed his eyes for a moment, lying against a solid branch as the wind whis-pered through the leaves around him. They were right in the middle of fae territory—the faery woods. Which meant they were fucked sideways.

Keeping his expression level and calm, he climbed back down.

Hope looked his way as he landed lightly on the ground. "All good?"

"Yep," he said confidently. "It's this way."

He walked off through a small clearing like he had a clue where the hell he was going. North, he decided. North was good. If his memory of the faery woods served him correctly, they were bisected by the Whispering River. If they reached that, he might be able to trade for a curricle and get them to the eastern trade route. It would be far safer for Hope that way.

As if thinking her name caught her attention, she jogged a few steps to catch up with him and looked up, her gaze direct and challenging for once. Most of the time she avoided looking directly at him or Claw. "We're lost. Aren't we?"

"Not at all. What gave you that idea?" he scoffed. They were, but he'd never admit it. First rule of survival as a half-breed was always look like you know what the fuck you're doing.

"We've passed that tree three times now. I broke one of the branches off."

His gaze cut to the offending bush to see the tiniest tip broken off. Shit, his Hope was clever. *Very* clever. Which was awesome but meant they had another problem.

Instantly, he feigned a relaxed posture, chuckling as he shook his head. "A stray breeze could do that."

Continuing walking, he herded her in front of him, expanding all his senses. He was an extremely accomplished tracker and warrior, and he hadn't had a clue they were going in circles. Which meant they had a huge problem. Magic was being used and it wasn't his. It was of a kind he wasn't familiar with and hadn't triggered his own, which meant it wasn't elven magic. He could smell the stink of that a mile off. No, this was something else. Something older and more dangerous.

So he kept his steps light and all his senses open, even as he itched to draw his blades. If something out here thought it was going to take his little human as a prize, it had another think coming...

CHAPTER FIVE

Hope had to admit, wherever they were, it wasn't horrible. But it certainly wasn't Haversham Park in the middle of a crowded city. Even taking into account the fact Graal was lost and they were apparently going around in circles, the ground they'd covered was way bigger than the park, even if she took into consideration the private section and its creepy looking house.

In fact, their surroundings were really quite pretty, she decided, watching a turquoise winged butterfly settle on a vivid pink flower nearby. She wasn't an expert in flora or fauna, but she knew enough to know that neither were natives of Earth. And if she wasn't on Earth, where was she?

"Not even a ruby slipper in sight," she muttered to herself, trotting to catch up with Graal's long-legged stride.

They were definitely lost, but her monstrous companion didn't seem to want to admit it. Hope sighed as she trudged along after him. Typical man, not wanting to stop and ask directions. Although, she had to admit, there *wasn't* anyone to ask out here. But still, she was sure that if there had been, he wouldn't have asked them. She seriously would never understand the male brain.

She glanced at him again, noticing the tension in his broad shoulders that hadn't been there before. "What's wrong?"

"We're being followed," he murmured, grabbing her arm and shoving her ahead of him. "*Run!*"

She didn't even manage to scream as the woods around them burst into life. The armored fae they'd seen on the road earlier exploded from cover with blood-curdling war cries, their faces twisted with hatred as they raised vicious weapons to hack at the trio.

Graal hauled her back as a glittering blade parted the air in front of her, almost taking her nose off, and he threw her toward a darker patch of trees.

"*Run!*" he bellowed again, and this time she didn't need any encouragement.

Head down and arms pumping, she ran like her life depended on it. Which it did. She was under no illusions about that. The loathing in their beautiful expressions had chilled her to the bone. She knew, without a shadow of a doubt that if she had given Graal the slip and approached them for help, she'd have breathed her last right there and then. Her head would already be on a pike somewhere.

The sound of clashing swords and screams behind

her made her run faster, tears snatched from her eyes by the speed of her flight. She shouldn't run. She should go back and help Graal... he was fighting them all on his own. She was a coward to run... she should go back and do something to help.

What? The sensible part of her brain demanded as the trees began to thin, the ground becoming rockier. She dodged and weaved between huge boulders, expecting to come face to face with a murderous fae warrior any second. *You can't fight. You're too small and weak. What could you do to help... apart from be a victim like you always are?*

The trees petered out, the woods giving way to a path into a rocky gorge ahead of her. Heart pounding and her lungs hurting as she tried to drag air in, she looked around wildly. There was no other way through. She'd have to take the path.

Her boots crunched on small stones underneath as she ran, her hair flying behind her. The screams and sounds of battle had fallen into nothing behind her. Trying not to think about that, she just concentrated on running, turning the corner to find herself in a valley with a glorious waterfall at the end. But she didn't have time to appreciate the beauty of the place, skidding to a halt as two fae warriors appeared on the skyline by the top of the waterfall.

With a gasp she plastered herself against a rock wall, tucking herself into the smallest crevice. Trying to calm her breathing, she prayed under her breath that they wouldn't see her. Her clothing was drab, nothing bright or fussy, so hopefully she'd just blend into the rock face.

Movement flashed in the corner of her eye and a second later a solid, heavy body pressed against her, almost flattening her against the hard rock. Something large and scaly crowded around her legs as a drooling muzzle shoved into her palm. She shuddered, in both revulsion and relief that they'd both made it.

"Hold still," Graal murmured as she got a face full of his chest hair.

The rough metal pendant he wore brushed against her cheek as he muttered something under his breath. She was about to ask what it was when she saw a flash of green. The sound of lyrical voices reached her ears and she stiffened, looking up into green eyes.

Graal shook his head, and she kept her mouth shut. She couldn't see anything past his broad shoulders, but the crunch of boots on the stone path along with the voices said they were getting closer and closer. Her breathing shortened. Any minute now they'd be discovered and—

The owners of the voices walked right on by, like they didn't see Graal's huge back to them at the entrance to the small crevice, raucous laughter indicating someone had cracked a joke. She kept her breathing as light as possible, not daring to move a muscle in case the fae doubled back and found their hiding place.

After what seemed like an eternity, Graal nodded and relaxed.

"It's okay," he murmured. "They're gone. Are you okay, little one?"

She nodded, dragging a shaking breath in as he eased back off her. Claw wriggled out from around her legs.

"I... I think so. I thought that was it. I thought they were going to kill us," she whispered, almost colliding with his broad chest again when he didn't step back as she expected.

Instead, he lifted a huge hand so that clawed fingers brushed her cheek oh so gently. "I would never let anyone or anything hurt you, Hope. You can trust me on that."

~

"*We need to put some distance between here and us before nightfall.*" That had been hours ago in the gorge, and Hope's feet were threatening not to talk to her anymore.

Graal walked faster than she could run, and she although knew he was slowing down for her, she could still sense his frustration that she couldn't go any faster. Occasionally he seemed to forget and leapt to the top of boulders the size of buses without thinking.

She admired the flex of thick horseman's thighs as he did, the length of his long, muscled legs bared by the little leather skirt thing he wore. She wondered if he wore anything underneath it, or whether that was just a Scottish thing. Probably just a Scottish thing... but it didn't stop her looking when he leapt to see if she could catch a glimpse of bare ass.

"So you're definitely not human," she said with a sigh as he jumped to the top of gargantuan fallen tree that blocked their path. Because they were cutting across country, he was having to create a path for them, most of the time with the huge machete sheathed on one hip. He carried a sword twice the size on the other. "Or you'd be aware that we cannot leap tall buildings in a single bound."

He looked down and a grimace twisted his features. "Shit. Sorry, I forgot you're tiny."

Leaping down, he scooped her up before she could protest. A squeak escaped her as he leaped, the air rushing past her face, and a second later they were on the top of the fallen trunk.

"Don't you dare drop me!" she warned breathlessly, clinging to his broad shoulders.

"Oh, so now my little lady *wants* to be carried, hmmm?" He grinned at her, a teasing light in his odd green eyes that instantly dispersed the dark mood that had fallen over them since the attack in the gorge. She was trying not to think of the sheer brutality Graal had shown. Thankfully, he'd washed the blood off in a small stream they'd passed.

"Yeah, well... unless you want to wait for me to climb small mountains each time," she replied grumpily, catching her breath as he leaped down from the trunk effortlessly and landed in a half crouch. He continued walking, still with her in his arms.

She tapped the back of his shoulder. "Errr... did you forget something? Like putting me down?"

He cut a sideways look at her and then shook his head. "Nope. You reminded me you're not orckin. You're small and delicate. I would not wish to wear you out with walking all this distance. And Karak always carries Kelly when he can. Unless they've had an argument, and then she's usually shouting and throwing things at him. Which makes it somewhat difficult for him to carry her."

Okay... that answered the question over whether the mysterious Kelly was a prisoner or not. If she was confident enough to shout and throw things, her "mate" probably wasn't holding her captive. It was a relief.

She latched on to the other thing he'd said instead. "Orckin? Is that what you are?"

"Aye, an orc." He looked at her oddly. "Wasn't the green skin obvious enough?"

"Well, it was obvious you're not human! Humans don't have green skin or white hair, not unless they're old. For all I know you could be an old troll or something!"

That seemed to nettle his pride, his head drawing back as he shot her an affronted look. "I am *way* too good-looking to be a troll. They are ugly, gnarled creatures with thick skin."

Ooooh... she'd found a trigger, and the little devil on her shoulder couldn't resist jabbing at it. "I bet they have bigger cocks, though."

His mouth dropped open, something flaring in his

eyes she didn't have a name for—something between utter fury and complete astonishment, with a side of frustration. She caught her breath, expecting his hold to turn cruel as she berated herself. Hadn't she learned her lesson with Harold and his sons? Never taunt someone bigger or stronger than you.

But Graal's hold didn't change. Instead, his jaw tightened and he lifted his chin. "One day you will see. My cock is massive and will bring you much pleasure. Much more than any troll's could. And they don't know what to do with their tongues," he added. "All they want is soft holes to fuck. No finesse."

She hid her fledging smile. Okay, he could take some teasing. Maybe not a lot, but his first instinct wasn't to lash out.

"Your hair is very nice, though," she admitted, gathering the courage to touch it. It was far softer and silkier than she'd expected. She'd thought it would be like wire, but instead it felt like cool satin under her touch.

"Thank you," he said, a little begrudgingly. "I wash it every few days and then condition it with a rinse of Althea root."

She blinked. He was into personal grooming? A monster... Sorry, an *orc* into personal grooming? The concept blew her mind. Harold and his sons primped and preened in front of the mirror, but she'd never thought anyone as manly as Graal would bother.

"Althea root is good for conditioning?" She had no idea what Althea root was, but it sounded fascinating and she wanted to keep him talking. On a subject that wasn't his cock.

He nodded, holding her in one arm as he slashed at the thick vegetation in front of them with the machete in the other. "Buttercup, one of the camp whores, collects it for me. If I pay her extra."

Hope stilled. "Extra? Extra on top of *what*?"

He kept walking, not meeting her eyes. "I pay her to fuck her. Anything else costs extra. She really fucking stings me for gathering Althea root and flat out refuses to kiss or cuddle. And I *know* she does that for Thorlack. The kissing and cuddling."

He speared her with a direct gaze. "And if she does that for one customer, she should do that for all of us. Shouldn't she? I mean that's only fair and I know for a fact that my cock is bigger than Thorlack's, so that should get me extra? No?"

"Men! You're all the same!" she hissed, fury filling her as she struggled to get free. "Put me down, you great oaf! I'd prefer to freaking walk!"

CHAPTER SIX

*H*ope was mad at him.

At least, he was fairly sure she was since she hadn't spoken more than a word or two to him since earlier this afternoon. He frowned as he selected a suitable clearing for them to make camp for the night and paced the perimeter to set wards. As his magic swelled, he searched his memory, trying to figure out what she'd gotten upset about.

Human females were very delicate and easily upset. He'd learned that watching Karak and Kelly. She seemed to take offense at the slightest, normal thing Karak did, which then necessitated many apologies from Karak. Graal had been incensed and horrified at the amount of groveling his friend and commanding officer had to do until Karak had clued him into "make-up sex". It was apparently hot and sweaty, rough sex that humans liked but not too rough given their more delicate statures. They wouldn't ask for it, though, so apparently they picked fights to get it.

He cut a glance to Hope, curled up against a large rock in his cloak. Surprise rolled through him. Was she... had she started a fight with him in the hopes of "make-up sex"? Heat rolled through his body, making his loincloth tighter. It would certainly seem that way since the only thing she could have gotten upset about was his mention of Buttercup earlier. Being annoyed a whore helped him gather grooming supplies *did* seem like a silly thing to start a fight over, but if the fight was about sex rather than Althea root... yes, he could see how it all worked.

His smile broadened as he gathered up wood for a fire. Normally he wouldn't risk it this far behind enemy lines as either the light or his magic to conceal it might give them away. But he hadn't seen any hint of fae in the area since the road earlier, and no creature moved as fast as an orc to cover distance. And with something else, something older and more eldritch in the area confusing his sense of direction, he would risk it. Most predators in the woods stayed away from fire.

Settling himself down on an old root, he set about starting the fire. He built it up into a small stack and then blew a spark of magic into the dried kindling to get it blazing in no time.

"Neat trick."

Hope's voice surprised him, and he looked up to find her watching him with fascination.

"Just a spark of magic." He shrugged. "Anyone can do it."

In truth he'd never really thought much about his magic. He was half orc and half elven, which meant he had more power reserves than most orckin—a fact that asshole Skali was always going on about, insisting that Graal retrain as a wizard. Why would he want to do that? His place was on the battlefield, his riven sword in hand, not on some hill somewhere making shapes with his damn hands and trying to pretend he was better than every other orc.

But he wasn't above using his power, here or on the battlefield. Many an elf had felt the broadside of his sword or a blast of pure power from his hand. Even though technically it came from the enemy, he'd long since gotten over that. There was a sense of irony using it against them.

"I can't. How did you do it?" She shuffled forward a bit to get closer to the growing fire. "I saw what you did and it kind of makes sense, like if I squint and look sideways I can figure it out?"

"Careful." He chuckled as Claw rejoined them, dropping a brace of hares at his feet. "You'll have the king's pet wizard after you if you talk like that. He's always saying it's just a case of us concentrating harder to master magic."

His smile faded as he reached down to pick up a hare, his sharp claws making short work of skinning and gutting it for the fire. No way would he let Skali anywhere *near* Hope. She was his human. That asshole wizard would just have to get his own.

"Ugh, that is so disgusting. How can you let him do that?" she asked, wrinkling her nose as he flicked the entrails to Claw to eat. The kregas nosed through the bloody mess, selecting the choicest organs to chew on happily as Graal set up the hares to roast on sticks over the fire.

He shrugged. "What do you expect me to do? Not feed him after he hunted for us? What he doesn't want will feed the earth here. Nothing is wasted. Is this not the way where you're from?"

She shrugged, looking discomforted. "You seem to live a lot closer to nature than we do."

He took that as a yes, settling down and stretching out his long legs in front of the fire. It was going to be a long night. Since there was only the two of them, he would have to pull a double watch. Which wasn't a problem. He'd done it so many times in the past on solo patrol, but this time it was different. He had her, his precious prize, to protect.

He studied her in the firelight. She was still kind of odd looking—small with delicate little features. Her eyes were wide and so dark he wasn't sure if they were black or brown. Her skin wasn't as pale as his, but he found he didn't mind that. The dark curls of her hair fascinated him. They weren't the lazy curls of the women in villages and towns the army often passed, achieved by rags in their hair as the women slept, but more riotous.

"So why does he like humans?" she said suddenly. "Has he met many?"

He looked up at her from where he was tending the fire to find her studying Claw. The hound had flopped over on his side, his belly to the fire to warm up.

"Kelly, my friend's mate, feeds him snacks and gives him scratches. He thinks because you're human as well, you'll do the same. Once he gets an idea in his head, it's hard to get him to let go of it.

She blinked and he could almost see the question crowding behind her eyes.

"Errr... I have some old candy, I think," she said, patting the pockets of her odd clothing.

Claw sat up, his eyes shining brightly in anticipation with one paw raised in plea.

Her hand disappeared into the folds of her clothing and when it re-emerged, Claw sat up straight as an arrow, his tail beating the dirt. Graal didn't blame him, even he could smell the sweetness from the object in Hope's hand as she carefully unwrapped it.

"It might be a little furry," she warned, her eyes on the kregas hound.

"He wouldn't care even if it had a pulse," Graal rumbled, turning the hares on their sticks. They were doing nicely now. He watched the little interplay between the human woman and the hound.

Claw's nose twitched and flared before he shuffled forward, extending his neck so he could sniff at the treat. She tensed, obviously expecting to lose a few fingers, but he sucked the candy delicately from them. It disappeared into his maw, barely chewed before he swallowed. The next moment she squeaked as the dog launched himself at her, and she found her arms filled with a wriggling, tail wagging, scaled dog.

"See, told you he liked you," Graal chuckled. "Okay... these are done. Ready to eat?"

He made sure she had the choicest cuts from the two hares, watching her tear into the meat with her blunt little human teeth. He still thought she was too small, but the body he'd pressed up against when he cast a camouflage enchantment over them in the gorge had been pleasantly curvy. So much so he hadn't been able to contain the natural reaction of his body. His cock had been hard and heavy in an instant, and had she been orckin, he had no doubt she'd already be riding him as a way of saying thanks for saving her life.

But humans didn't seem to follow the same rules of courtesy. She hadn't even offered to suck him off. He grumbled to himself as he threw the remnants of their meal to Claw when they were done and settled down on his side of the fire. The camp was warded, so no fae would stumble across them, and the fire would keep anything darker away. He would keep watch anyway, maybe catch a few catnaps when Claw was awake. Kregas were normally nocturnal, so the hound was often awake and alert during the night, a fact he and Karak had used to their advantage a few times.

"Is it going to get much colder?" she asked suddenly, shivering even though she was wrapped in his cloak.

"Probably."

He lifted an arm, hoping she trusted him enough to cuddle up next to him. "Come. Sleep here. I'll keep you warm."

Eyeing him warily, she shuffled closer. Closer and closer until, finally, she settled in next to him. Sighing in contentment, he wrapped his arm around her and pulled her in tightly.

"How long does it normally take humans to get ready in the morning?" Graal groused as he waited by a small stream as Hope splashed about in the water behind him.

"That depends on how many coffees I've had and the availability of decent bathroom facilities," she snapped back, obviously not a morning person like he was.

Wanting to get a good start on the day, he'd woken them all early, but rather than the smile he'd expected from the little human, he'd gotten a snarl and a curse he was fairly sure wasn't anatomically possible. He'd practically had to unroll her from his cloak in order to get her moving. And even then, he'd had to wrestle her for it.

She was surprisingly strong for such a small female.

"And so far, we're zero for two—no coffee, no bathroom. So I'll be ready when I'm god damn good and ready. Understand? Now keep watch please. And no peeking. It's bad enough that your damn dog is perving on me. I don't need you doing it as well!"

Graal just grunted in reply with his arms folded over his massive chest. His little human was very waspish this morning. Perhaps he'd picked a bad one? Kelly had always seemed to be of a sunny disposition in the morning, so he'd thought all humans would be that way.

His brows cleared of their frown. But... Kelly was regularly serviced by orc cock. Perhaps that was it...

"You seem out of sorts this morning, my little petal," he said over his shoulder. "Perhaps riding my cock will make you feel better."

"What?" The splashing stopped suddenly. "No. Why the hell would you think that?"

He shrugged. "It seems to make Kelly feel better. I'm prepared to give it a go if you are."

"You sleep with your friend's wife?"

The low dangerous tone of her voice gave him pause.

"What is it? Like some green-skinned free-for-all orgy or something?"

Even her incensed tone couldn't stop his bark of amusement at the idea of Karak allowing anyone near his beloved mate.

"By the tusk, no! Karak would rip my cock off and shove it down my throat if he suspected I'd ever even thought of Kelly that way."

"Good. Someone needs to keep you in check. You're entirely too obsessed with this whole cock riding business," she said stomping past him to put her boots on.

He was disappointed to see she was fully clothed again and wrapped in his cloak against the chill of the early morning air. When she said she needed a bath, he'd thought that maybe finally she'd found her manners, and at least he'd get to ogle her tits or something.

But no, she'd barked at him not to peek, and now she was fully dressed. He sighed. It was a complete letdown.

"Why wouldn't I be?" he asked, watching her lace

up the heavy boots. She had the tiniest feet imaginable. He'd known humans had tiny little feet without claws. Kelly had shown hers off in delicate strappy heels that had definitely made him uncomfortable in the loin-cloth region. But Hope hid hers in big ugly boots. "I have one of the biggest cocks in the orc army."

She should be begging him to let her ride it, but so far... nothing. Humans were very strange indeed.

"Yeah, yeah." She tied her laces off with a vicious yank and stood. "So you said several times. You do know there are other ways to flirt than boasting about your equipment. Right?"

"Yeah, of course." He folded his arms over his chest. "I am an excellent flirt."

"Sure you are, handsome." She smirked. "Now did you get me up at the crack of dawn for the fun of it, or are we getting out of here sometime today?"

He paused, watching her. "You think I'm handsome?"

Finally, she was starting to see sense!

"Seriously? *That* was your takeaway?"

He watched in surprise as she stomped off, Claw hot on her heels. If that wasn't bad enough, the hound eyeballed him every step of the way.

"Damn kregas." He growled at him. "You soon showed where your loyalties lie. Didn't you? A little bit of a snack and you're all *human, human, human*. Aren't you?"

He stomped behind them, bringing up the rear, and made sure his sword was loosened in its sheath. They walked until the sun was high in the sky, passing nothing other than a few bumblebees and deer who watched them with limpid eyes.

His hands itched for his bow. They were such easy marks, obviously unafraid. Noticing the way Claw's tufted ear twitched, he smiled. The kregas had noticed them too... which meant they would have venison for dinner tonight.

Despite the relatively easy night's rest they'd had—nights in the Enchanted Woods were a lot easier than on the Northern line—he hadn't forgotten that they were behind enemy lines. That fae death patrol had managed to track them without him being aware of it, which rankled his professional pride. Something about this place interfered with his senses and made him want to sneeze all the time. He didn't like it. Not one bit.

His jaw tightened and he gritted his teeth so hard he was surprised his tusks didn't shatter. They wouldn't get the drop on him again, though. That was for sure. He was onto their sneaky little tricks, like making him go around in circles.

"Wait up. I want to check something," he called out, looking up at a solid oak. It was the tallest tree around. Using his claws, he hauled himself up to the lower branches and then climbed as high as he could to check the position of the sun in the sky. It was very crude method of navigation, but at the moment, it was the only one he trusted. At least the sun was a constant that the fucking fae couldn't alter.

"Oh, how beautiful, Graal. You have to come and see this."

He frowned as he dropped lightly to the ground,

turning just in time to see Hope walk under a rose-covered archway that had definitely not been there before he'd gone up the tree. Through it, he could see a pretty cottage with a rocking chair outside, and a small fountain splashed musically. The hairs rose on the back of his neck. It all looked so good that he knew instantly it was as wrong as wrong could be.

"Hope, no!" he bellowed, launching himself toward her.

But it was too late. She stepped through the arch and disappeared. Exchanging a look with Claw, he roared as they ran toward it. Orc and hound barreled through the archway after the pretty little human.

CHAPTER SEVEN

The instant Hope stepped through the archway, she realized she'd made a terrible mistake. The beautiful music she'd heard emanating from the cottage—harp music or something of the like—became harsh and discordant. It hurt her ears as she stumbled forward. Catching herself mid-stride, she did a double take as she looked at the cottage.

It wasn't as bright and clean as she had first thought with a neat thatch and red shutters open to reveal fluttering curtains.

Instead, it was dirty and looked abandoned. Half the thatch was gone, revealing the bare rafters of the roof reaching up to the sky like the ribs of the decaying skeleton, half picked over by predators.

Most of the shutters were hanging off their hinges, the once bright red of the paint faded to the color of old blood. The curtains were little more than dirty rags hanging limply in the windows.

She backed up, her hand over her mouth as the

smell of rot and decay assaulted her nostrils. This was wrong, all kinds of wrong. But before she could turn and flee back through the archway, the dead vines training across the yard whipped up and wrapped around her ankles.

She gasped and jerked to a stop as the thorns from roses long dead bit through her jeans. They ripped into her skin, climbing their way up her legs and body to wrap around her wrists. A hiss escaped her as they bit into soft skin, trails of blood marking her skin to drip to the ground. She had the awful feeling the dirt beneath her feet was *hungry*.

"Now, child. Didn't your parents teach you it's bad manners to leave without saying hello?"

She jumped as an ancient voice cackled by her ear. Her heart beating a rapid tattoo against the inside of her ribs, she twisted to see who was speaking.

A wizened crone walked around Hope, her eyes beady and bright over a hooked nose as her tattered black robes fluttered in the breeze. Lank, dirty grey hair hung greasily over her shoulders. Hope blinked, hardly believing her eyes. If there was an award for archetypal evil witch who lived in the woods, this woman would win hands down. She even had a hairy wart right on the end of her nose and a gnarled wooden staff to lean on.

"No. Didn't yours teach you that it's wrong to tie people up?" she snapped back, at the end of her tether with this whole ludicrous situation.

Not everything that is pretty is good, pumpkin.

"Pay attention, child!" the crone snapped her long,

gnarled fingers in front of Hope's nose. She even had long, blackened fingernails any stiletto false nail aficionado would die for.

"Hard not to when you asked so nicely. Which finishing school did you attend because your manners are exquisite," she threw back, not at all concerned that she might anger the old witch and get her face eaten off. "There's not enough coffee in the world for this shit. Now what do you want since you went to all this trouble to get my attention?"

The crone eyeballed her. Like literally crowded into her personal space and shoved her wrinkled old face into Hope's.

"Oh, you're a brave one. Aren't you? Pretty too."

Hope was not at all brave, or at least she didn't feel it. Right at that moment, despite her bravado, her knees knocked together so loudly it would give a woodpecker envy, and a cold sweat slithered down her spine.

Circumspectly, she tried to look over her shoulder. Where the hell was Graal? He should have been right behind her.

"Expecting someone, my pretty?" The crone trailed long fingers through Hope's hair, making her shudder.

"My companion," she said, glaring the witch down. With her hands caught behind her back, the only weapon she had in her arsenal was her glare. "He was right behind me, and believe me, you do *not* want to be here when he gets here. He's big and gree—"

"Green with silver hair and tusks?" the crone finished for her and then smiled. Her teeth were surprisingly less decayed than Hope had expected.

"Yes dear. I know all about Graal Orcson."

She clicked her fingers and Hope's two companions appeared, hanging upside down from the nearest tree branch and wrapped in vines. Graal struggled as soon as he saw her, fear in his eyes. She winced as thorns sliced through his green skin causing rivulets of scarlet to run down his body and stain his silver hair.

Her gaze snapped back to the crone, a fury she'd never known before simmering through her veins. She'd never stood up to anyone before, but that was back home. This was an entirely different world, so why shouldn't she be an entirely different Hope?

"Let them go!"

"Ahh, I might do!" The old woman cackled. "But first you'll have to do something for me, Howl's Hope."

She froze, watching the old woman warily. "How do you know my name?"

"Secrets and shadows." The crone tapped the side of her nose with a gnarled finger. "Both mine to know..."

More riddles. Hope gritted her teeth. "What you want me to do?"

"So quick to agree... Didn't your parents teach you better?"

Hope sighed and leveled a hard gaze on the woman. Her mother had always called it her evil look, saying she'd gotten it from her father.

"Look, lady, that's the second time you've questioned my upbringing. Don't make it a third. Now you obviously called me here for a reason given that neither Graal nor spot over there could see your little archway trap until after I did. Which means you wanted me specifically. And given I'm not from around here..." She looked around at the woods around them pointedly.

"Then that makes me think that whatever you want, you need a non-local to get it. And, for the record, I didn't agree with anything. I just asked what you wanted," she added. "No agreement was given nor implied. Now, I'll ask one last time. What the hell do you want?"

~

*W*here had his little human mouse gone?

Graal had never seen anyone stand up to a witch with such courage and determination before. The few true witches he'd met—and the swell of power in the air told him they faced a true witch— had such fearsome reputations, but most people would have run the other way as fast as their legs would carry them. They certainly wouldn't have looked down their noses with disdain, like she was the witch queen herself, as Hope had just done, and demanded the release of her companions.

It was exhilarating, impressive as hell and, he was forced to admit, hot as fuck. Which was a bit of a problem given the fact that, in his current position, his loin cloth flat lay against his stomach rather than hid the very impressive evidence of his arousal. Which was not a position he really wanted to be in when stuck upside down in a witch's lair.

Twisting, he kept his eyes on Hope as she stared down the witch. If that evil female hurt her, he didn't care how long it took or what he had to sacrifice. He would find her and make her pay.

"What I want... What I want?" the witch mused. "Now that really is the question. Is it not, my dear? Power. It's always about power. I would have thought you'd have realized that with the power running through your veins."

Graal frowned and looked at the witch in surprise. Power? What power? Humans were nulls. They had no magic in their veins. Karak's mate Kelly had proven that when she'd nullified the faery bomb the assholes had sent into the main orc camp.

"I have absolutely no idea what you're on about, crazy lady," Hope declared. "But I'll play along. What power do you want that I can get for you?"

Graal's blood ran cold in his veins. *No, no, no*, never ask a witch something like that. His little human would find herself on an altar stone bleeding out her heart's blood so the witch could harvest the power she claimed Hope had.

"Oh, my dearie... What are you offering?" The witch crooned as she stroked long fingers over Hope's throat.

Graal bellowed, the sound muffled by the vines that gagged him as he thrashed about, trying to get free. Beside him, Claw did the same. A low ominous snarl trickled from his bound muzzle as he picked up on Graal's tension. Then Graal noticed that the kregas hound's gaze was fixed unwaveringly on Hope.

That in itself was not a surprise. Kregas were fiercely loyal, choosing their companions carefully, and he'd always assumed that Claw had bonded with

Karak. But the hound's dedication to Hope made him wonder... And then there was the old tale that Gunther Howl's great-grandfather had tamed the very first kregas. They were all supposed to be loyal to the Howl bloodline.

"I'm not offering anything, but I promise you I'll take that hand off at the shoulder if you don't stop touching me," the human warned the witch with a growl that would have made any orc proud.

To Graal's surprise, the crone snatched her hand back like she'd been burned. "Very well, my dear, since you are so eager for information. I need pips from an apple eaten by the Queen of Summer herself."

"Wait, what? That's it?"

Graal thrashed even more, trying to get her attention. The Queen of Summer was an old—very old title —for the faery queen. But his attempts to get Hope's attention were fruitless.

Instead, she just laughed. "I thought you were going to ask for something rare or expensive."

He closed his eyes. What the witch wanted was neither rare nor expensive, just fucking impossible. No way in the realms could they sneak into the faery court, grab an apple core, and get out of there without being seen. No way at all. He was totally the wrong color for a start off.

"Do you agree then, my dear?"

"Yes. Where does this Summer Queen live?"

As soon as Hope agreed to the witch's terms, the vines wrapped around Graal and Claw loosened. He grunted as they dropped, managing to get his arms up over his head before he landed on it. He knew he had a thick skull, but he wasn't particularly fond of landing on it.

He and Claw landed in a tangle of limbs. Flipping over, he tore the vines from over his mouth.

"Hope, no! We can't go to the faery court!"

She blanched. "But we're not. We're going to the court of the... Summer Queen?"

Her eyes narrowed in suspicion and she rounded on the crone.

"Who is the Summer Queen?"

The witch grinned broadly, making sure to stay on the opposite side of Hope from Graal as he strode over, ripping vines off as he went.

"The Summer Queen? Why... she's the child of spring and the mother of autumn."

Hope sighed and frustration washed across her face.

"Let's try this again," she said, her tone long suffering. "Are the fairy queen and the Summer Queen the same person?"

Surprise rolled through Graal as the little human challenged the witch. How she knew to ask a direct question and not give at the crone room to wriggle, he had no idea, but she did. She'd removed a lot of the witch's power right there and then.

An innocent look passed over the witch's wizened and wrinkled face.

"Well..." she wheedled in a nasally voice. "Not really. She's changed a lot since she was called that... so she might as well be an entirely different person."

Hope's expression set. "So if she's a different person, that means the Summer Queen no longer exists, and our agreement is now concluded."

Surprise flashed in the crone's beady eyes and Graal hid his grin. Hope had her there.

"Wait... No, that's not how it works."

"That's exactly how it works. You can't break your own rules," Hope said, folding her arms.

Power swelled in the clearing as the witch's face darkened thunderously. She lifted her hands, probably to turn them into toads or something. Graal winced. No way were they getting out of this, no matter how many fancy words Hope threw at her.

"So if you want us to travel to the *faery court,* you're going to have to provide us with the means to get into and out of the court successfully," Hope added.

The witch flicked greasy hair back over her shoulders, but the tension in the clearing eased to a bearable level.

"And why should I do that? What's in it for me?"

Graal opened his mouth to warn Hope not to agree to anything else. It was bad enough that they had to go to the faery court without adding any extra conditions or side quests. The little human shot him a warning look, giving a small shake of her head.

"Because an agreement made under false pretenses is null and void and shows a duplicitous nature. Besides..." She gave the witch a look that would have frozen hell over twice.

"*They* are both free, and you still need me to get the apple, which I *will not do...*" Hope raised her voice as several vines slithered across the undergrowth toward him and Claw. The kregas hound growled and snapped at the vines that came near him. "...if you tie them up again."

The witch clicked her fingers and the vines fell lifelessly to the ground.

"Very well. I will accede to your request." Reaching inside her robes, she pulled free a small bottle, the green fluid glowing within.

Holding it out to Hope, she said, "Walk down the path until you reach the briar roses. Then drink this... a little each. It will give you what you need to travel to the court and back."

"Safely?" Hope asked suspiciously, holding it up to look at it.

"Perfect!" Graal reached past her to grab the bottle in one huge, clawed hand. "Thank you so much. We're just going now."

Grabbing Hope under the arm, he hustled her away down the path. "Keep walking in case she changes her mind and turns us all into frogs or something!"

CHAPTER EIGHT

"We had a lucky escape. That could have gone much worse," Graal muttered in a low growl as they left the clearing and the witch's cottage behind. "At least she didn't eat our faces off or try to cook us in her oven."

Hope still couldn't believe that her talking back to the witch had worked and they were free and clear. She smiled at his words and looked up at him as they walked down the path in the direction the witch had indicated.

"I think witches only cook children, and besides, you're entirely too big to fit in an oven. At least, unless she had an oven big enough for a rhino. But..." She cast a glance back over her shoulder. The woods had already swallowed up any trace of the witch and her cottage. "Her cottage wasn't made of gingerbread so I think you're safe anyway."

The confusion on his face was highlighted as his brows snapped together.

"She was the wrong type of witch," she clarified.

He shot her a quick look, surprise and what looked like dawning respect in his eyes. It was like she'd finally done something that surprised and impressed him. "You have training in witchlore?"

"Of course. Doesn't everyone?" she said lightly, not admitting that her "training" came from the fairytales she'd loved as a child.

She remembered bedtime stories with her father. Being tucked up safe and sound as he told her fantastical tales of mythical creatures and daring heroes. Of princesses who dueled with dragons and evil witches who wanted what they had. She hadn't realized until she was much older that her father's tales were different and way more embellished than any in traditional fairytale books, but she hadn't cared. His stories had always been more interesting.

"Indeed not," he rumbled, slowing down to match her pace with interest in his eyes as he looked at her. "That kind of knowledge is highly prized and controlled by the king's wizard, Skali."

She frowned, the name prickling at something in her memories, but before she could poke at it, the path widened out. Ahead of them was a small gate with rose bushes on either side. She had no idea if they were briar roses or not, but they were the only roses around here, so they would have to do.

"This is definitely it," she announced, eyeing the gate. Not only was it an obvious end to the witch's property, but it felt different, like she could actually feel the edge of the witch's magic. She shivered, shaking her shoulders to get rid of the odd feeling.

Lifting the potion, she looked at it. The fluid swirled and sloshed about inside, like it had a mind of its own. Little sparkles floated around in it, like tiny fireflies dancing in the viscous fluid.

"Oh my, it's a real magical potion," she breathed.

An eye appeared on the other side of the bottle, blinking myopically. She lowered it to come face to face with the big monster.

"Did you expect it to be something else?" he asked mildly. "The real question is what it going to do to us."

It was a good question. A damn good question. She looked at it again.

"Well, given that she needs us to get something for her, it's probably not going to kill us?"

He arched an eyebrow. "Probably?"

She shrugged, feeling a bravado she hadn't known back at home. "Only one way to find out, isn't there?"

Unstopping it, she put it to her lips and tipped her head back. The potion hit the back of her throat like that one time she'd stolen a nip of her stepfather's whiskey. It stole her breath and burned all the way down to her stomach.

Lowering it, she extended her arms and checked herself over. Nothing. No extra legs or anything. She didn't look or feel any different.

"Anything?" she asked, looking up at Graal. He stared at her, his expression stunned. "Yeah? Did something happen?"

He blinked, clearing his throat. "Yeah... you're...

fuck, you're beautiful. Utterly fucking beautiful like this."

The warmth that had started to spread through her chest stuttered to a stop.

"Like this?" Her voice was light, covering the hurt that spread through her system like wildfire.

He nodded, taking a step forward as his gaze roved over her and then fixed back on her face. "You look... fuck, I've never found a fae attractive, but you're stunning."

"O...kay." So he only found her attractive when a spell had changed her appearance. Talk about an extreme makeover. "Back it up, big boy."

She held out the bottle. "Your turn and then Claw."

He shook his shoulders, snapping out of his trance, and took the potion. Lifting it, he sipped carefully. She tried not to watch, fascinated despite herself at how his tusks worked. They protruded from his lower lip line but they didn't seem to get in his way. She'd wondered if he could actually chew or whether he just tore at his food, but she'd watched him last night eating. His other teeth seemed to be in line. Only the tusks were different.

He swallowed, strong muscles moving in his throat, and then, before her very eyes, his appearance changed. He morphed from a huge, green-skinned monster into an equally huge, silver haired, stunning looking...

"You look like an elf," she said, hiding her smile.

He blinked, his hands shooting up to his face and to his mouth.

"My tusks... they're gone," he said, surprise in his voice. It was still deep, but somehow more melodic now. Definitely a singing voice.

"Your eyes are like... a moss green now," she said, performing an investigation of her own features. Like Graal, she hadn't changed height or body shape, but her hair... She blinked as she studied the long, blonde strands... her hair had totally changed color and—

She froze as her hands reached her ears. They now had delicate points to them.

"Oh my god, I have pointed ears!" she squeaked softly. "Real pointed ears."

"And they are very, very cute ears." He grinned, crouching down and motioning to Claw.

"Come on, sunshine. We need to do something about those scales."

The hound sniffed warily at the potion bottle in Graal's hand, sliding a quick look at Hope. She smiled in what she hoped was reassurance. It must have been because his scaled butt hit the dirt and he opened his mouth.

"Good boy," Graal crooned and tipped what remained of the potion down his throat. He swallowed and then growled and sneezed explosively, shaking his head.

Between one shake and the next, his scales disappeared with a pop and the biggest wolfhound she'd ever seen sat in his place, tail wagging.

"Hey, handsome boy." She grinned, reaching down to scratch behind his ears. "Don't you look great!"

"He won't look out of place at court, either," Graal

said, ushering them both through the gate and off the witch's territory. "Let's get out of here. Shall we? Hopefully this enchantment will hold up long enough for us to get there, get the apple, and get out. Otherwise, we're utterly fucked, and not in a good way."

~

"Why did you tell the innkeeper we were married?" Hope hissed as a maid led them upstairs to their room.

He leaned in to reply, his voice low so only she could hear. "Because high elven ladies do not travel alone unless they're in the queen's army. Anything different is suspect and will be reported. Now... We're newlyweds, remember? Giggle," he ordered in a low murmur and then kissed the side of her neck.

She was so surprised that she gasped, and then her brain kicked in and she giggled while leaning into him. He was large, warm, and smelled so good that she moved closer, fitting herself against his side.

She'd wondered at his change in attitude since they'd left the witch's garden. With their changed appearance and the new clothes that had appeared with the witch's spell, they'd been able to travel on the main road and had made good time, reaching this roadside inn just before nightfall. She'd caught the looks he kept sending her way—a mixture between confusion, appreciation, and outright lust. He'd also stopped talking about his cock... she wasn't sure if that was a good sign or a bad one.

"Boss put you in here, my lord," the serving girl said, holding a door open. She somehow managed to avoid looking at Hope completely.

She wasn't quite an elf, but at the same time, she definitely wasn't an orc like Graal. Hope thought it best not to ask, just in case she outed herself by not knowing something that was common knowledge around here.

"Water jugs are already heating on the fire," she smiled, looking Graal up and down appreciatively. "Just ring the bell if there's... anything else I can do for you, my lord."

"Thank you, *we* certainly will," Hope replied waspishly, grabbing Graal's hand and yanking him into the room after her. The big orc had to duck to avoid hitting his head, and Claw followed on their heels, still looking like a huge wolfhound. She was pleased to note that the serving girl gave the hound a wide berth.

"God, can you believe the nerve of that woman!" she hissed as soon as the door closed behind them. "She practically propositioned you right there in the corridor! I thought she was going to drag you off and have her way with you in a cupboard or something."

Stomping across the room, she flopped on the bed. Then she groaned and flipped over.

"Oh my god, I love you," she said, her voice muffled by the soft bedding. After being on their feet for the last two days and sleeping on the ground last night, lying down on a soft surface was utter heaven.

"Do you think so?" Graal's voice had an absent tone, and she looked up to find him lifting one of the big metal jugs to start filling the bath. As he poured, more and more water flowed from it, steaming as it filled the huge wooden tub.

"Perpetual replenishment spell," he said when he caught the direction of her gaze. "Damned difficult to cast, therefore expensive. I'm surprised an inn like this has them."

"Probably because missy out there is too busy flirting with the male guests." Hope sniffed, looking at the tub again. It didn't look like it would take long to fill.

She wandered around, almost stepping over Claw who had spread himself out on the floor next to the bed and had promptly fallen asleep.

The room was larger than she'd thought, and the furniture was like something out of a fantasy film. All carved wood and homespun blankets with cotton sheets that looked so inviting if she wasn't dirty from the road, she'd have burrowed into them already.

Then she blinked, turning to shoot an accusing look at Graal. "There's only one bed."

He looked up, strong hands still holding the ever-full jug steady. "Yeah... what did you expect? I told them we were newlyweds. This is what counts as the bridal suite around here."

She arched an eyebrow. "Right, and you had to tell them that because... reasons. Sure. I'm onto you, buddy. You get the floor tonight."

He shrugged, a small grin flirting with the corners of his lips. They looked... kind of odd without his tusks. But that was probably because she was so used to seeing him with them, she reasoned.

Then again, she looked different as well. She leaned forward to study herself in the mirror on the dressing table.

"This potion is absolutely amazing," she murmured.

The woman who looked back was her but not her all at the same time. Her hair had been transformed from its normal dark brown curls to blonde shot through with strands of shimmering silver, but her eyes were still her own, dark brown. Her skin was amazing, clear and soft, like it was living its best life here in the fresh air and nature.

Her ears fascinated her the most, though. Pulling her hair back gently, she studied them. She'd always loved stories of elves when she was a child and had often pretended to be an elven princess from one of her father's stories—beautiful, wise and brave, ready to defend her kingdom from all threats.

She frowned as the memory came to her clearly. How odd, always before her memories had been of generic princesses, and if she'd been pushed, she'd have named a princess from a recent book or film. But this memory was different... she had always pretended to be Riana, the Spring Princess before she became a queen. And that sounded like something more from here than back home.

Shaking her head, she put it down to interference from the witch's spell. The crone had put the idea of seasonal queens in her head. That's what it was. Her memories were old, and after her father had died, there had been no more stories, no more games.

Sadness had reigned supreme in the Howell household until Harold had arrived and charmed his way into her mother's heart. Thankfully, she'd been old enough at the time to realize that Harold would never be her father, and as a teenager, she hadn't wanted one.

She had hoped he would at least make her mom smile, but within a year her mother had been gone as well, leaving her to Harold's tender mercies.

She sighed. If ever she'd needed to be strong and capable like Riana, it had been then and the years since as Harold and his sons bullied and belittled her into nothingness. Until she was nothing but a pale shadow of her former, childhood self.

"They're not going to drop off, you know?" Graal said from across the room as he finished pouring hot water into the tub.

"Best get in while it's hot," he said. "I can't use my magic to keep the water warm."

Moving away from the window, she looked at him with curiosity. "Why not?"

He hadn't said anything about his magic, and she'd just seen that one hint of it last night when he'd started the fire to cook their evening meal.

He stripped his shirt, folding it and placing it carefully on the trunk at the foot of the bed, giving her the opportunity to ogle his heavily muscled shoulders and chest. He didn't have an ounce of fat on him. Before the spell, she'd seen several old scars dotted over his green skin, evidence of a hard life on the battlefield. They were gone now, leaving smooth, satin skin her fingers itched to explore.

Down, girl, she scolded herself as she started to undo the laces on her gown. Fortunately they ran down the front, so she didn't have to worry about getting Graal to unlace her. Score one for female independence, even in a fantasy world.

Her hands slowed as Graal reached for his belt buckle.

Her voice emerged as little more than a squeak, "What the hell do you think you're doing?"

CHAPTER NINE

Graal glanced up to find the little human looking at him with something akin to horror. It wasn't the expression he was used to seeing on females' faces, and he found he didn't like it. Not at all.

"I'm getting in the bath," he replied, undoing his belt.

Perhaps she'd taken a hit to the head in the witch's clearing that he didn't know about? A bath sat in front of them, and he was taking his clothes off. It should be obvious to her what he was doing.

"Uh-uh." She shook her head, backing away from him. "We're not going in the bath together. You'll have to wait."

His hands froze on the fasteners to the fancy breeches provided by the witch's spell. Trust the damn crone to have picked the most complicated fasteners she could think of.

"Seriously? You won't bathe with me... even though the water will go cold?" He blinked. "I did not think humans were so selfish. Or so prudish."

"I..." Her cheeks turned ruddy as she glared at him, her eyes flashing with fire. "And I'm not selfish. I'm just not used to sharing a bath with anyone. It's not... we don't do things like that at home!"

Her ire was adorable, and he was hard-pressed to hide his smile.

"You must be very wealthy to afford to bathe alone then," he said and continued undressing. He wasn't shy about his body, either his real form or this pretty elven version of it. "I am not trying to seduce you, merely to get clean."

Removing his breeches, he draped them over a nearby chair and turned to step into the tub. She watched him, like a rabbit frozen by lamplight. Then her gaze wandered downward. A chuckle escaped him as she squeaked and squeezed her eyes shut.

"I can't believe you're actually doing that!"

"Having a bath? I might even go wild and use the soap next."

He was teasing her, but he couldn't help it. She wasn't scared of him, which was nice. Even though he wasn't as scary as Karak or some of the other orcs in the army, he was still an orc, which meant most females were actually more than a little scared of him even as they invited him to their beds. It was the reason he stuck to paying Buttercup and her colleagues.

She also wasn't *treating* him like an orc, he realized,

but like an actual person instead of a ravening beast who could tear her limb from limb with the slightest provocation.

"You can get in," he said in a low rasp, seeking to reassure her. "I'm in the water. Perfectly decent."

He didn't know why he said that. He didn't *want* to be decent. He wanted her gaze on him and to see her reaction to the sight of his cock again. It had only been semi-hard, nowhere near its usual impressive size and length, but she'd still gasped, her cheeks flaming a deeper shade of scarlet.

Perhaps she really *had* never seen a male before? He'd never had to be careful of a female's sensibilities before. It was... new.

She cracked an eyelid and squinted at him in suspicion. Like she expected him to be standing in the tub, cock in hand as he whirled it about. When he wasn't, she sighed and eyed the water with longing.

"Okay. It's a big tub. You'll have to look away."

He chuckled, lifting his arms and resting them across the side of the tub. "Now why would I do a thing like that?"

She arched an eyebrow. "You want me to march back to that witch and tell her I changed my mind?"

He sighed, rolling his eyes. Human females had no sense of humor. "Fine."

Leaning his head back, he closed his eyes. Silence reigned for a few moments, and then the soft rustle of cloth filled the room. He'd intended to peek as she stepped into the tub, as he had for countless other females he'd bedded, but this time he found he couldn't.

Instead, all his other senses were on high alert as he imagined the gown sliding from her shoulders, revealing that soft skin that had been tantalizing him since the moment he'd met her.

He hadn't been able to work out what her figure was like beneath the shapeless human clothing she'd worn, but the witch really had done him a favor by replacing them with the green and gold gown. In the current style of the faery court, it skimmed her mouth-watering figure and had had him half-hard all afternoon.

Now she was undressing *right* in front of him, and he couldn't even take a peek. He sighed. Sucked to be him, and not in a good way.

"You really should consider my cock. Many females have ridden it," he informed her, pulling his shoulders back so she could admire his physique.

Water splashed followed by a rippling around him, which said she'd gotten in. He risked opening his eyes to find her sitting primly opposite, the water lapping around delicate shoulders. She was so tiny and fragile he felt like a ravening beast next to her. He *was* a ravening beast anyway, but she never made him feel like it.

"You said that before." Her lips pursed. "I'm still not sure how you think telling me that you're a male tart is going to persuade me to fuck you."

He frowned as he tried to put the words into an order that made sense to him. Then he blinked.

"You think it was a boast?"

He was across the tub in less than half a second, the water sloshing around them as he reached out to take her hand in his.

"It was not," he said, trying hard to convince her he was in earnest. "It was to reassure you than I am a talented and skilled lover. My cock will bring you much pleasure."

Her lips parted on a small gasp as she tried to yank her hand back. He wouldn't let her, instead wrapping his much larger hand around her delicate little one. He could *make* her do what he wanted... she was so tiny and delicate, no match for his strength.

With an effort, his bones practically creaking, he released his grip so as not to scare her.

"I..."

This wasn't like him, not at all. He was the suave, sophisticated one among his brothers. Where they resorted to grunting and beating their chests with their conquests, he *talked* to them. So why couldn't he talk to this tiny little human?

He gave up and moved suddenly, leaning in to claim her lips in a soft kiss. She started, water splashing up against his chest as she put her little hands there to push him away.

Only she didn't. Her hands stayed there, just resting on the hard planes of his chest as he took a chance and kissed her again. Not hard, no tongues, and he didn't wrap an arm around her, crushing her against his bigger, currently *very* hard body, even though he wanted to.

Instead, he braced his hands on the sides of the tub, holding his body away from hers. He was still so close he could feel the heat of her skin against his, and she could touch him if she wanted to. Slide those little hands down the front of his body—

He groaned against her lips. They were the softest things he'd felt in his life, and he knew he'd never get enough of kissing her. Soft and pliant, they were a little slack at first, impassive.

But she didn't scream or slap him across the face. It gave him hope as he tilted his head, exploring the shape of her little mouth and the curves of her lips.

Then... in a move beyond his wildest expectations... she began to kiss him back. Softly at first, so softly he wasn't even sure her lips were moving, but then as they parted a little and he felt her tiny exhale against his lips, he knew.

He couldn't help the rumble that escaped him, the wood of the tub creaking under his grip as he forced himself to stay in place as she kissed him back.

It wasn't the most erotic kiss he'd ever participated in, but it rocked him like no other and left his breathing ragged when he lifted his head to meet her startled brown eyes.

"Don't think this means you're sharing the bed, Monster."

~

S he'd kissed an orc, and... well, hell, she'd liked it. *Really* liked it.

The next morning Hope's thoughts were still fixated on *that* kiss in the bathtub. It had been almost innocent, no tongues, but it had scorched her right down to her soul. She also suspected it had affected Graal just as much.

She slid him a little look over her shoulder as they rode down the road. Somehow he'd organized a horse for them, so now she practically sat in his lap, trying and failing not to think about the massive cock he kept boasting about as they rode toward the palace of the fairy queen. Claw had left them earlier this morning, dispatched back to the orc camp as they approached the court. The illusion hadn't taken as well on him, and they couldn't afford for him to pop a scale and blow their cover.

Graal hadn't attempted anything beyond the soft kiss, which had surprised her. Especially considering they'd both been as naked as the day they were born in the water. But he hadn't.

Instead, he'd pulled back when she thought he'd press his advantage. The rest of their bath, and the evening, was uneventful. They'd shared a meal in front of the fire in their room, the table and chairs appearing magically as the maids had arrived with their food.

It had been good, but she couldn't remember anything they'd eaten. She'd been too tired to do anything after that but tumble into the embrace of the soft sheets where she'd slept like a baby until this morning.

"You keep looking at me. Do I have something on my nose?" Graal rumbled, his broad chest brushing against her back. She suppressed the shiver that wanted to roll up her spine. At least he was dressed now, rather than half-naked like before.

"No... sorry. I was wondering how you slept?"

She felt guilty for making him sleep on the floor while she took the comfort of the bed. Well, she *hadn't* at the time, on account of her falling asleep as soon as her head hit the pillow. He'd been gone from the room when she woke, giving her time to... attend to business and be dressed again before he returned with some soft pastries and apples for breakfast.

"I'm sorry for hogging the bed. I meant to swap halfway through the night but I didn't wake up."

That had been a surprise. She didn't sleep well normally, always waiting for footsteps outside her door.

He looked down, surprise in his green eyes. They were a softer hue now, more moss colored. "There's no need to be sorry. I was more than comfortable."

She blinked. "How? You slept on the floor!"

A deep chuckle rumbled up from the center of his chest. "I was warm, dry, and no one tried to kill me. It was a good night."

She couldn't say anything to that. It was a little window into the brutality of his life—one that his scars and the well-worn condition of his weapons, now rendered into an approximation of elven weaponry by the witch's spell, hinted at.

"Don't you have... like a home?" she asked, wanting to know more about him. He hadn't talked much about himself or where he'd come from last night, mostly asking about her.

"Home? Like a building?" He shrugged. "I've always been with the army, from as far back as I can remember. Whelped in the camp nursery and got under a lot of feet before I was big enough to pick up a sword."

This time she did turn around, looking at him over her shoulder in surprise. "You mean you've been with the army since you were a kid? I thought you said your mom was elven?"

"Yeah..." He gave her an odd look. "But I never met her."

"How do you know she was an elf then?"

She was definitely missing something here. And by the expression on his face, it was something obvious.

A grin split his face. "Apart from my stunning good looks and this, you mean?"

He flicked his silver hair over his shoulders like he was in a shampoo commercial. It was the only part of him that the witch's spell hadn't altered.

"Yeah..."

"I can sing," he admitted, his expression serious. "Most orckin can't. Only those of us with elven blood."

"So you never knew your mom? I'm sorry."

She had only good memories of her mother, apart from the time she was ill, and she'd give anything to spend five more minutes with her. But for Graal to have never known his...

He shrugged. "I'm not. Most half orcs are either

drowned at birth or left out in the wilderness. If we're lucky, we're found by scouts and brought back to the camp."

"What... they abandon their babies? How could they do that? I would *never* abandon my baby. Not ever."

She'd always wanted to be a mom, always wanted a family she could call her own.

His gaze locked on to her, laser focused. "What? Even if that baby had green skin and tusks?"

An image of Graal as a baby popped into her mind, tiny and unwanted, left out of his own in the wild. Her heart ached. Anything could have happened to him.

"Yes, of course! Why wouldn't I?"

She frowned as she turned, looking ahead again. *Could* she love a baby orc? The image in her mind changed to a little boy with her dark curls and Graal's green eyes, and her heart lurched. Could she... her and Graal?

"A baby is a baby," she said firmly. "They all deserve love and someone to care for them."

His arm tightened around her waist, and he settled her closer against him. "You are a rare female. Your children will be lucky to have you as their mother."

They rode in silence for a few minutes. The road since the inn had been quiet so far but now the traffic was beginning to build up.

She tried to study the other travelers on the road without them noticing. She hadn't seen any other humans. Everyone she saw had that ethereal otherness that had marked the elves and the people at the inn.

Either that or they had wings, horns... or other extras that marked them as different.

"So, there aren't a lot of humans here, are there?" she murmured to Graal, careful to keep her voice down. The witch must have disguised her as an elf for a reason. "Are humans rare?"

"Yes and no," he replied, gathering the reins and urging their mount to the side of the road to allow a convoy of wagons to pass them by. "Humans have always been considered a myth. Well, until Kelly fell through the mists and we realized you were real."

"So you used to have humans... if we were a myth."

He nodded, waiting until the last wagon had passed before taking up the center of the road again. "Humans were once numerous in the realms, ruling several of the ancient kingdoms."

"What?" Surprise filled her. "How? Did we have magic? Otherwise, we'd be the bottom of the pecking order."

Birds chattered in the trees around them, forcing Graal to wait to answer as a winged woodcutter crossed the road in front of them. He cast them a curious look but didn't comment as his gaze landed on the sword strapped to her companion's hip.

"No, humans are nulls. They can't access elemental magic in the same way as orckin and the fae. Instead, they mastered the *ene'thai,* the power that exists in the spaces between everything, the power that makes up the world itself. Their sorcerers are still spoken about in whispers today."

"Oh wow... But none of them survived?"

He shook his head. "No one knows why. Some bloodlines claim human blood and can wield the *ene'thai,* but the most they can do is cheap parlor tricks, nothing like the legends of old."

They reached a turn in the road, and she gasped as a fairytale castle loomed up over them.

"Now quiet, female," he grunted. "We approach the court."

CHAPTER TEN

As an orc, Graal had never entertained any ideas of visiting the court of the faery queen. The only time he'd ever thought about being here was as an attacker, when the orc army invaded the enchanted woods and took the palace by force. So he studied the layout of the castle walls with a warrior's eye as they approached, noting the number of guards and their positions.

The castle itself appeared to be constructed of pink-veined marble, beautiful in the midsummer sun, but he knew that was only an illusion.

At the moment the battlement walls were low enough that the bottom of the banners hanging from them brushed the wildflowers in the meadow that surrounded the castle. The main gates stood flung wide open to admit the streams of visitors approaching from all directions. More were here than he'd expected.

Had they been an invading army, the meadow would have dropped into the depths to become a deep moat, the walls stretching themselves up to the sky and becoming impenetrable granite.

Most people didn't realize that the castle was a part of the enchanted woods and just as alive. It could change its appearance at will and was the main and most dangerous part of the queen's defensive forces. According to the legends, invaders weren't safe once they got past the battlements and into the interior either. In fact, they were in more danger as the castle led them down blind corridors to trap them in rooms without doors or between walls. It made the court virtually impenetrable.

But for now, the castle was welcoming and unthreatening as they rode through the main gates.

"This is utterly beautiful," Hope breathed in front of him, thankfully keeping her voice barely audible. "It's a real fairytale castle."

"Careful, beautiful," he murmured, his arm tightening around her waist protectively. "Here even the walls have ears. Literally. The entire palace is a fae construct.

"Really?" She twisted in his lap to look up at him, her eyes wide. She was so adorable, all he wanted to do was kiss the breath out of her like he had last night.

Despite his words to her that he'd passed a comfortable night, in reality he hadn't. Instead, he'd barely slept. After that kiss he'd lain awake, listening to her soft breathing in the bed next to him.

In times past, he would have charmed his way into the bed with her, silencing her protests with kisses. It was all part of the taken by a feral orc fantasy that many town matrons and village maidens had going on.

But with Hope he just couldn't do it, and he had no idea why. At first he'd thought maybe the witch had done something to his cock with her spell. Which—if she had—would have caused large-scale grief across the realms from the many females who had declared themselves in love with his cock. But wrapping a hand around his shaft and thinking of Hope's soft lips under his had disabused him of that notion almost immediately. It had only taken three tugs before he spilled his seed all over his own stomach, the climax so explosive he'd lain there shaking with his heart pounding as he stared up at the ceiling.

So, he mused to himself, he didn't have a cock problem. He had a Hope problem. She was impervious to his charm, which was both exhilarating and frustrating as fuck all at the same time.

"Good afternoon, my lord... my lady," a stablehand appeared as they rode into the main courtyard of the palace and came to a stop. "May I take your horse?"

"Of course." Graal dismounted in a single, fluid move and waved away the squire hovering to help Hope down. The lad was young, a mere twig of a lad he could have twisted into knots without breaking a sweat. Especially if he kept looking at Hope that way... in combined awe and base lust. Graal recognized it as the same way he felt about the beautiful little human female.

Not that she looked like a human with the witch's glamour over her. Instead, her glorious dark hair had been turned silver blonde by the spell, and she had delicate little points to her ears, but he was pleased that her eyes were still the same.

"I got this, kid," he rumbled, far too much of his real voice in the sound. But the squire didn't seem to notice, still staring awestruck up at Hope. Graal had to physically get between them to snap him out of it.

"Of course, my lord," he murmured, moving back with a deferential bow.

Graal turned to Hope, reaching up to fit his hands around her tiny waist. She weighed almost nothing as he lifted her from the horse, only letting her slide down the front of his body a little. She gasped anyway, her gaze flying to his and her cheeks coloring. He bit back a smile. She wasn't as unaffected by him as he'd thought.

Once he'd set her on her feet, the squire stepped forward.

"Please, my lord, my lady. Let me show you to your room," he said, indicating the main door of the castle with a sweep of his arm.

The deferential treatment from the squire and the other staff they passed made the hackles on the back of Graal's neck rise. If they could see beneath the witch's glamour to the real color of his skin, they... no, *he*... definitely wouldn't be welcomed. Hope would be safe—the fae had had no argument with humans—but his head would decorate the battlements between a couple of those fancy banners before night fell.

"A light repast will be served in your room this afternoon," the squire said as he led them up a set of winding stairs and opened a door to one of the tower rooms.

Hope gasped and moved past him, delight written on her face. "We've even got a balcony! Look at that view!"

"My wife is from the Dioneas region," he explained to the hovering squire. "This is her first visit to court."

"Very good, my lord." The expression on the squire's face was carefully neutral. Fae were volatile creatures, quick to anger, especially the nobility. "In that case may I suggest that your lady wife rest this afternoon. The queen's champion is expected to arrive back at court this afternoon, so tonight the queen will hold a ball in his honor. It is expected to go on until the early hours, probably later."

This matched with the rumors Graal had heard. The queen was notorious for throwing long balls, and protocol dictated that none of her guests could leave before she retired. On pain of execution. Some guests had actually died of exhaustion after dancing for days.

He inclined his head as he held the door open for the squire to leave. "My thanks, we'll make sure to do that."

Closing the door behind the young fae, he turned to Hope with a wicked grin.

"Whatever will we do to pass the time?"

ope's breath caught in her throat as Graal stalked toward her, intent in his eyes.

"I..."

Her words dried up in her throat as she backed up. Her heart thundered, but it wasn't because she was scared of him. Far from it. She was aware of every move he made, and the wicked darkness in his eyes.

Her back hit the wall, leaving her with nowhere left to go, but she didn't try to escape. Instead, she watched him, heat simmering through her veins and her knees weakening as the memory of his lips on hers filled her mind.

"Cat got your tongue, beautiful?" he murmured as he reached her, planting his hands on either side of her head on the wall as he leaned in.

He didn't touch her, only the coolness of his breath washing over the side of her neck, but she couldn't have moved. Not pinned by his darkened gaze the way she was.

"I'm more than capable of talking, *Monster.*"

She threw the old taunt at him but her voice was too soft and sultry for it to mean anything. It had ceased to be an insult long ago anyway, and in that instant they both knew it.

"Really?" he rumbled and leaned into her. Not hard, but enough that she felt every muscle in his hard body, the heat of his skin through her dress... and the beat of his heart against hers. "Sure about that?"

She registered the hard bar of his cock pressing

against her and her eyes widened. Oh my god... he hadn't been joking about his size.

"All I've been thinking about all morning is kissing you again," he murmured, leaning down and brushing his lips over hers. She gasped at the slight contact, sharing her breath with his.

Her eyes sought his, the expression there making her ache in ways she'd never have expected. Not for him... for a monster with green skin. But all she wanted him to do was kiss her again. To pull her into his arms and kiss her so she didn't know where she ended and he began.

"You want me to..." He teased the corners of her lips with his. "You know you do."

She nodded, rising onto her tiptoes to kiss him back. But her lips didn't meet their intended target. He moved, stretching up to press a stone in the wall high above her head.

The squeal of stone scraping right next to her made her jump, and as she turned toward it, a section of the wall opened up to reveal a doorway with blackness beyond.

Graal gave a wicked grin and grabbed the torch from the wall. "Come on then. Let's go exploring."

She was left looking at his broad back as he disappeared through the doorway. Her breathing still ragged, she gathered up her skirts and hurried after him.

"Where are we going? How did you even know that was there?"

Thanks to the torch, she could at least see where they were going. The narrow stone corridor led to a tiny staircase. She didn't need to be an architect to realize it was hidden in the walls of the tower and probably ran on the outside of the stairs they'd walked up with the squire.

"What are these? Old servants' corridors?" she asked, taking Graal's arm as he offered it to help her down the steps.

The torchlight glinted off his eyes, for a moment turning them back to their natural, yellow-green color. An odd pang of... something rolled through her when the spell reasserted itself and they turned moss-green again.

"No." He shook his head. "I don't think so. The entrance was concealed with magic, and we saw servants on the main stairs earlier. No. This is a proper secret corridor, probably for spying on others."

He put his fingers to his lips as they reached the bottom of the stairs and another long corridor. They saw patches of light up ahead, but she didn't see any torches. Only when they were almost on top of them did she realize what they were.

"Spyholes," she breathed. "Actual spyholes."

Motioning to Graal to pick her up, she grinned as she looked through one. Sure enough, it showed the room beyond—a bedroom and with a woman asleep on the bed.

Hope didn't say anything after Graal had put her down and they'd hurried past the spyholes into a darker section of the corridor.

"But why for spying?" she asked, keeping her voice

low just in case. "This is a fairy castle. Why not use magic?"

He shrugged, the fine lawn of his shirt moving over one massive shoulder. "For the same reason I found the door. Everyone here has magic so they'd sense it. Sometimes the best way to defeat magic is by *not* using magic. Gods, what I'd give for some parchment and a pen to make notes on the castle layout."

She blinked up at him, surprise rolling through her. "You can read and write?"

He frowned. "Of course I can. What do you think we are? Animals? We're taught as children. Aren't you?"

She shut her mouth with a click, realizing she'd made assumptions based on his appearance, and nodded.

"Quiet now," he warned as the corridor opened out ahead of them. "I think we're approaching the main hall of the castle... the throne room."

She nodded, sliding her hand into his free one. It was a little odd to feel his fingers without the claws she knew were there. How had the spell done that? It was even more impressive than turning her nearly black hair silver blonde. She knew women back home who paid a fortune for the same effect.

He glanced down at her in surprise and then his hand tightened around hers slightly in reassurance as they crept toward another set of spyholes.

These she had no problems looking through because they were set lower, forcing Graal to crouch. When she peered through one, she realized why. They were set to look through some kind of tree sculpture, the spyholes positioned so the watcher could look between the branches and the leaves.

The splendor of the throne room was laid out before them. The throne itself was on a large dais to one end of the hall, opposite the large double doors that were nearly half the height of the cathedral-style ceiling. She craned her neck, trying but unable to see right up into the shadows of the high vaults.

"My champion, so good to see you finally returned to us!" a feminine voice called out, and the queen herself walked into view. She was everything Hope had imagined a fairy queen to be, all silver-blonde beauty with wide, innocent cornflower-blue eyes. Her own narrowed. It was easy to see why she had once been called the Summer Queen. She gave off an aura of warm, summer days and sunlight... and it left Hope utterly cold. She shuddered, trying to dispel the chill that wanted to wrap around her just looking at the fairy queen.

"It is an honor, as always, to be in your presence, my queen."

An elf approached from the open double doors, his voice deep and booming. He was dressed like a knight, in chain mail and armor, his long, dark hair cascading over shoulders that were broad for an elf. She couldn't help comparing him to Graal in his normal form. The elf definitely came off worse in that comparison. Plus, he gave her the same cold feeling that the queen had. She didn't like him on sight, probably the type who tried to grope waitresses.

A woman trailed in his wake, her cloak hood pulled

up to conceal her face. She was tall and slender, and something about the way she moved seemed familiar.

"Of course. It always is." The queen clapped her hands and demanded imperiously. "I trust you have brought me a present, Lord Naebalar."

"Spoiled much?" Hope muttered softly, which got an answering soft snort from Graal next to her.

"That's fae nobility for you," he replied softly, his voice pitched to carry to her ears only. "They think the world revolves around them."

"I have indeed, your most gracious and beautiful majesty," the champion announced, turning behind him to look back through the doors and clicking his fingers. "I caught this foul beast near the northern border and thought it would make an excellent centerpiece for the celebrations. We could hold a tournament for the right to slaughter it like the animal it is."

Yeah... fairies weren't at all nice, Hope decided, her jaw tightening as she watched four fae soldiers drag in a chained man covered in fur.

Her breathing caught as he straightened up, the fur cloak falling back to reveal green skin, long black hair, and heavy tusks much larger than Graal's.

An orc. They'd caught an orc.

"Fuck!" Graal breathed, the shock clear in his voice. "That's Gudvar!"

She turned suddenly, looking up at him, and her foot must have caught a rock. It tumbled and hit another. The sound was tiny but they both froze. Graal's hold on her arm tightened and she held her breath.

"What was that?" Lord Naebalar demanded. "Is someone else here?"

"*Move,*" Graal breathed, shepherding her back up the corridor ahead of him. When she didn't move fast enough, he picked her up, half hauling her over his shoulder as he pounded up the stairs.

Before she knew it, they were back in their room as the door slammed shut behind them.

She looked up at him as he put her down. "Who is Gudvar?"

Graal paced the room, shoving a hand through his hair. "It's a long story. He was my father's battle partner."

"Was?"

He nodded. "My father died before I was born, but everyone knew I was Braestak's kid..." He motioned to his face. "It's written right here."

"So he's like your... uncle?"

Graal snorted. "Fuck no. He hates my guts. Says my dad chasing after an elf got him killed, so somehow that was my fault."

She sat on the edge of the bed, watching him. It was easy to see he was rattled. "So... what are we going to do? Leave him to his fate?" She didn't like the idea of that, but she also didn't know anything about the orcish culture. Perhaps being captured was like a big dishonor or something...

He looked at her like she'd grown two heads.

"We're going to rescue him, of course."

CHAPTER ELEVEN

Graal had had many reasons for coming to the faery court, but the fact that the witch had put a compulsion on them to do so was the least of them. He had a rare chance to spy on the court and its goings on, which he couldn't pass up. And now he had another complication. Namely getting Gudvar out of here.

He had no idea what had happened and how the big half-troll had managed to get himself caught. Unlike some orcs with troll-blood, Gudvar was cunning and quick-witted, too clever to be caught by the usual type of trap the fae used.

Leaning against one of the pillars in throne room, he watched the guests at the ball as they whirled, danced, chattered, and generally enjoyed themselves. They were a mix of elves and fairies, with some other, minor fae as well.

He'd even seen a couple of fae from the dark court, but he made sure to stay far, far away from them. Of all the guests here, they were the most likely to see through the witch's enchantment and realize what he really was.

At least, he *should* be watching the guests. Instead, he was mostly watching Hope as she hovered around the buffet table nearby. The queen wasn't far away, outfitted radiantly for the ball in a gown of spun silk and gold, her crown atop her head. She was basking in the adoration of the group around her, a half-eaten apple in her hand, but the fruit was the only interest Graal had in her.

For one, she had wings, which made him shudder and for a second... His gaze slid to the little human ready to pounce if the queen put the apple down. To him, Hope was far more beautiful.

He blinked, thinking about that. For years, he'd envied the beauty of the fae, seeing echoes of it in his own movements and features. It was like seeing something and never being able to quite touch it. And when he'd first met her, he'd thought her odd looking. Not tall enough, too curvy... her features odd. But now he wanted to scrub the false beauty of the witch's spell again and see her proper, human features.

"You need to be more careful," a beautifully soft, lyrical voice said right by him, almost startling him out of his skin.

An elven woman stood at his side, a wine glass held elegantly. And elegant was the only word to describe her. Tall, nearly as tall as he was, she had silver hair that reached to her waist and pale green eyes that studied him seriously.

"I beg your pardon?" he asked, straightening up. If this woman wasn't high fae, he'd eat his hat. "I'm sorry, my lady, I don't think we've been introduced."

"Indeed not." She smiled, the expression enigmatic as she took a sip of her wine, looking at him over the rim of her glass. Her eyes seemed strangely familiar somehow. "My name is Adharian, Lady of Sharnwood Heights."

He blinked. Lady Adharian was—

"Yes, I'm the champion's wife."

Her tone was dull and stilted as she looked across the hall to where Lord Naebalar was holding court with a bevy of admirers. Two younger fae women were hanging from his arm, and both would be sharing his bed tonight if Graal didn't misread the guy's body language.

"It was not a marriage of my choice, before you ask."

He hadn't but he nodded anyway.

"I'm sorry, my lady. If that is the nature of your interest in me, I am myself happily married," he said, nodding toward Hope by the buffet table.

"Oh, by the leaf, no!" Her laughter rang out in a beautiful melody as she patted his arm. "No, I am not trying to tempt you into my bed. That would be... problematic since I knew your father."

Graal forced a polite smile to his face. "I think you might have me mistaken for someone else, my lady."

She took a step closer, the smile dropping from her face. Her voice was low, the expression in her eyes urgent and focused as she studied his face. "No, I do not think so. You are the very image of him, but his hair was black as midnight. His left tusk was broken at the tip."

He froze, watching her face. This was a test. It had to be. There was no way an elven lady, no less than Naebalar's wife, an elf well-known for his hatred of the orc race, had just revealed she knew an orc. Knew *his* father.

"He was so beautiful," she carried on. Her expression softened and he knew she was looking into the past. "Fierce and brave. My father and his men were away when I found Braestak, injured in the woods."

He nodded, not sure what he was supposed to say. If this was a trap, anything he said could be used against him. But how could she know what his father's name had been?

"I nursed him back to health, as best I could and..." She looked away, color on her cheeks. "We were in love. He promised to come back for me."

Oh shit. He knew how the rest of this tale would go. Many women had... *relations* with orcs, but mostly it was a onetime thing. Even if not, a relationship between an orc and an elf? It was a nonstarter.

"I'm sorry," he said, reaching out to touch her arm soothingly. "Some things are just not meant to be."

She smiled, and he caught the unhappiness in the backs of her eyes before she shuttered her expression.

"I bore a babe that summer, with the most beautiful green skin and eyes. Silver hair like mine," she whispered, looking up him like he was the sun, moon, and stars combined. "When my lover didn't come back, I left him beneath a willow tree on the riverbank."

Shit. He'd been found by an old scout beneath a willow tree, in a bark crib.

Was this his... mother?

She smiled at his startled expression, but before she could say anything else, a harsh shout from across the hall made her look up.

"My apologies. I am summoned," she said, her expression shuttering over the spark of hatred at the sound of her husband's voice. She looked back at Graal.

"You don't need to say anything. I don't know why you're here, but please, please be careful."

He nodded slightly, still wary. If questioned he could always say he was just humoring the crazy lady. She half turned but then stopped, looking over her shoulder.

"I waited, you know, just to make sure someone found you. I couldn't leave you on your own... so I waited until someone came. Until you were safe."

And with that, she was gone, leaving him looking the way she'd gone in utter and dumbfounded shock. All these years he'd thought his mother had abandoned him to his fate. But she hadn't... he *had* been wanted after all.

~

She'd always loved tales about fairy balls, but she'd never actually thought she'd get the chance to attend one. Hope lingered around the buffet table, pretending to be interested in the fairy cakes while ignoring the irony of their existence. They even had little wing decorations.

While she perused the delicacies on offer, half of which she had absolutely no chance of identifying, she looked around without trying to gawk. That was not the easiest thing in the world to do when there was so much to marvel at.

It was like something out of a film, or the fairytale books her father had read to her from when she was a child. The beautiful illustrations of fairy ladies in their beautiful dresses and handsome elven knights had held her spellbound, so much so that even now, as an adult, she swore she remembered seeing them move. The illustrator must have been a master at their craft... she just wished she could remember what the book had been called. She'd never seen another copy like it, no matter how many antique bookshops she'd visited.

The ball was the same as the pictures, the ladies in beautiful dresses of all colors of the rainbow. Torches were lit all around the throne room, the side wall of the castle somehow gone to reveal a wooded clearing with fireflies dancing in the branches. The light glittered off the glorious jewels around the necks and in the hair of the ladies in attendance.

It was beautiful and awkward all at the same time, especially when she had to take the wings into consideration. Like shimmering, ethereal capes, several times she'd almost walked into a pair when the owner suddenly snapped them open, often looking at her in irritation. She wasn't used to dealing with people whose personal space extended so far. So she avoided them to prevent any more possible faux pas, noticing that most people gave anyone with wings a wide berth and never approached them from behind. Like a horse who might kick without warning.

She noticed a few outlandish costumes, but she managed to keep her expression level. A real elven lady would probably be more than used to all this, and she didn't want to out herself inadvertently. Not when the witch had done such a good job of helping them to blend in.

She had to admit, her skirts swishing about her ankles as she moved about the table, seemingly absorbed in making her selection from the multitude of cakes on offer, that the witch's spell was amazing. So far it had adapted hers and Graal's clothing for each situation they'd found themselves in. When they'd been traveling, it had clothed them in expensive but hardy attire that suited their cover of an elven lord and lady, but earlier, when she'd been freaking out about what to wear for a court ball, it had come through again. With a slight tingle of magic, her traveling gown had reformed itself into a sumptuous black and gold ballgown, complete with tiny slippers on her feet. She felt like a fairy princess herself.

Even though she knew at least two *real* fairy princesses were in the room, she didn't care. She felt like one, and in the safety of her own mind, that's what she was.

Reaching the end of the table, she picked up another little cake for the growing collection on her plate and looked about the room, concealing her interest in the queen talking to a small crowd of devoted admirers a few feet away. Queen Oonais was talking animatedly, waving a half-eaten apple about in her hand. It was so enticing to see their prize right there that it was all Hope could do not to grab it as she ran past and make a break for the door.

She still hadn't gotten the image of Graal's friend in chains out of her mind, nor the bruises and cuts marring his green skin. A shudder hit her. That could easily be Graal in chains, a thought that made her blood run cold.

She didn't know much about magic. What would happen if the witch's spell wasn't strong enough and failed? They would be revealed, and Graal could be hurt along with his friend. The very thought made her feel sick.

She looked over to the last place she'd seen Graal to reassure herself he was okay and unhurt, and her breath caught in her throat. He was surrounded by a little group of fairy women, two with wings and one without. The wingless one looked up at him, a hand on his arm and a sultry look on her face as she went up on her tiptoes to whisper something in his ear. The easy smile and answering expression on his face made it plain to see that the woman had done the fairy equivalent of telling him her room number.

A small growl escaped the back of Hope's throat unbidden. "Fucking little hussy," she muttered under her breath, throwing a few more cakes on her plate without even looking at what they were.

Tinkling laughter met her ears and she glanced

back at the queen in time to see her throw the half-eaten apple core up in the air and clap her hands. At the sound, the core erupted into a flock of cerulean-winged butterflies

"Fuck it," Hope hissed, seeing her chances of nabbing their prize today fly off into the trees. Grabbing a last cake, she stormed across the hall to where Graal was surrounded by his little groupies.

"Sorry, ladies," she all but snarled, hip-checking the wingless little hussy trying to move in on her man. It wasn't a hard hip-bump, but given that the average fairy seemed to weigh less than a paper towel, the woman almost ended up on her ass on the floor. "This one's taken. Go find another bed-warmer."

And with that, she dragged Graal's head down with a hand on the back of his neck and kissed him soundly.

He groaned, his lips parting under hers as his hands slid around her waist. Pulling her up against him, he tilted his head and kissed her back.

She lost all sense of space and time, her arms sliding up and around his neck. She didn't care where they were or who was watching. All that mattered was kissing Graal, which she did with all the pent-up frustration in her soul at watching others flirt with him. He was *her* monster, not theirs.

Her toes left the ground, and she lifted one foot behind her as his big hand cupped her neck. A small whimper left her as his tongue parted her lips and drove within. She'd never been kissed with such desperate passion before.

"Hey... get a room! Or a tree! Some of us have been married far too long for shit like that!"

A joking voice broke the spell between them, their breathing ragged as they both pulled back to look into each other's eyes.

Graal looked as stunned as she felt.

"We need to get out of here," he murmured, his voice a deep landslide of a rumble that would have given him away for sure if anyone had heard him as he pulled her deeper into the shadows of an archway.

She grabbed his shirt, trying to hold him still as she pressed against him. "We can't leave before the queen. Remember?"

His gaze shot across the hall toward the queen. *"Fuck!"*

She giggled. "Yeah, I think that's the idea."

He turned back to her, focusing in on her like a hawk. "Say that again. Are you saying you want to... with *me?*"

She gave a small nod. She'd rather thought the kiss would have been obvious enough. "Do you see anyone else here?"

A horrible thought froze her in place. What if he *didn't* want to? What if all the talk about his cock had been just that... talk. Dropping her hands like she'd been burned, she tried to back up. Her cheeks were red as she stammered, "I mean, of course. You probably don't want to. I'm not really your type—"

His hold tightened, and he yanked her back up against his solid chest with a force that stole her breath.

"Oh no," he breathed. His eyes darkened in a way

that made heat simmer through her veins. "You're not getting away from me that easily, beautiful. Not after that."

She wanted to melt against him, but a prickle on the back of her neck warned her that they were being watched.

"Graal... later," she hissed, putting a little distance between them. "Not in front of everyone!"

He didn't let her get far, capturing her hand and putting it on his arm. They promenaded slowly around the room until the band in the corner struck up a tune.

"Dance with me, my lady," Graal leaned down to whisper in her ear, and before she knew it, he was pulling her toward the dance floor.

"Graal! No!" she squeaked, trying to pull on his arm, but it was like trying to stop a landslide. She ran to catch up with him, pulling urgently on his hand.

"I can't dance!" she hissed, panic filling her as she looked around.

Each man on the dance floor had taken his partner up into his arms, and they moved with the kind of elegance Hope knew she could never achieve. Her entire dance repertoire consisted of solo performances in front of the cracked mirror in her bedroom. She'd never danced in front of anyone, never mind *with* anyone.

"I can. Don't worry," he murmured and swept her up into a dance hold like a professional dancer. Before she knew it, they were whirling around the dance floor, Graal easily controlling her movements so it looked like she knew what she was doing.

"Relax," he murmured. "Enjoy it."

"What if I stand on your foot?" she whispered back, and he tightened his arm around her waist.

"I would suffer terribly, but it would be worth it," he shot back, a teasing twinkle in his eyes.

The laugh bubbled up out of her, a tinkling sound of amusement as she let go and allowed herself to enjoy just dancing with him.

He was an excellent dancer, and the feel of his big, hard body against hers hiked her heart-rate. She could understand why they called dancing the language of love. There was just something about moving against him, with him like this. Like making love while standing up and clothed.

So immersed was she in the fantasy, her gaze locked onto Graal's, that she didn't see the other couple whirling into her peripheral vision.

The first she knew about it was when something almost slammed into the side of them. Graal instantly half scooped her up and took the impact on his big, solid shoulder.

"Watch where you're fucking going!" he snarled, holding her protectively.

"You were in the way!" the other guy snapped back, and Hope's breath caught. It was the queen's champion. She recognized him easily from last night. Her gaze flicked to the woman with him, easily tall enough to have been the woman in the hooded cloak.

She was stunning. Tall and slender, she had the kind of ethereal grace that Hope had always envied on women who had it. She was too short and clumsy to ever be considered graceful. In fact, tonight in Graal's arms was the first time she could ever have described herself as having any kind of grace, and even that was borrowed.

"My lord," she murmured, a hand on the champion's arm. "It was an honest mistake. Please, let's continue our dance."

"No! This country oaf needs to apologize. He was in our way," the champion snarled, looking Graal up and down. His nose turned up like he'd smelled something suspicious.

"I do believe the floor rotates clockwise, Lord Naebalar?" Graal replied, his voice mild with dangerous undertones. "Unless tradition has been overturned and it has not reached our ears out in the provinces..."

"No, no... you are correct," the champion's partner replied, her hand still on the enraged elf's arm. "We were in the wrong. Our apologies. My lord?" she asked, her voice like steel.

A small crowd had gathered around them. Like sharks, they sensed drama like blood in the water.

Lord Naebalar snatched his arm away from the woman's touch. "The queen requires my presence," he snapped and stalked off.

An odd expression crossed the woman's beautiful face, and she dropped into a curtsy. "Once again, my apologies."

And with that, she was gone.

Hope looked up at Graal as he swept her up into the dance again.

"What on earth was all that about?" she whispered, trying to look over his shoulder to see which way the couple had gone.

He shrugged. "No idea. Naebalar's an utter prick. Always has been."

Glancing down at her, he whirled her into a turn at the edge of the dancefloor, dipping her over his arm with a heavily muscled thigh pressed between her legs. She gasped, heat flooding her system.

God, he was utterly devastating and so, *so* dangerous.

A bell rang out across the hall, and he looked up, a wicked grin spreading out over his lips. She missed his tusks, the smoothness of his lips a little odd after getting used to him with them.

She twisted to see what had his attention just in time to see the queen leaving on the arm of a very handsome elven knight.

"Saved by the bell," he murmured as he scooped her up against his chest and strode from the hall.

CHAPTER TWELVE

Graal didn't speak as he carried her through the corridors of the castle, his jaw tight as he climbed the stairs toward their room.

Not anger, but a different sort of tension stretched between them as he shouldered the door open and then turned, somehow closing it and pinning her against the back of it in the same movement.

She gasped at the feel of his huge, hard body pressed against her. He was either hard, and totally aroused, or he had a mace in his pocket. A *big* mace. Need and desire flooded her at the thought, liquid heat escaping her.

"Last chance, little one," he growled, big hands reaching for hers. They closed around her wrists like manacles and he pulled them out to the side. "Otherwise, I'm going to fuck you like only an orc can."

"Ssssshhh," she warned him. "Walls have ears. Remember?"

"Let them hear." His voice held the edge of a snarl,

his lip curling back in such a way she could almost see his tusks again. It was as if the sexual tension between them had interfered with the witch's spell for a second. "They won't take you from me. You're *mine*. You have been since the moment I saw you through the mists."

The possessive declaration made her knees weaken, and the heat in her blood rose to an inferno.

He seemed to take her silence as an answer, pulling her hands up over her head to pin them there as he leaned in.

"*Mine,*" he growled and then claimed her lips again.

This kiss was nothing like the ones before. When he'd kissed her before, he'd been careful and gentle as he explored and tested her reactions to him.

But now, sure of her response, he kissed her like he owned her. Parting her lips with a hard sweep of his tongue, he drove in, demanding her response with a dominance that thrilled and aroused her like nothing else.

She moaned, arching against him as she kissed him back. She wasn't entirely an innocent. She'd had a few relationships over the years, but none had lasted long before Harold and her stepbrothers had managed to scare them off. However, none of them had ever kissed her like this. Nor had she ever reacted to any of them with such need and desperation.

He broke the kiss, his order a harsh rumble, "Bed, now..."

Pulling her away from the door, he continued kissing her and backed her up across the room. She let him, sliding her now free hands over his chest and shoulders as she explored the huge, hard body she'd wondered about since seeing him in the tub last night.

He rumbled approval in the back of his throat, twisting and turning as he shrugged out of his shirt en route. She bit her lip as he broke the kiss for a second to pull it over his head. A second later his lips were on hers again and the back of her knees hit the bed.

He didn't push her back onto the soft surface like she'd expected. Instead, his kiss slowed and he pulled away to look down at her.

"This is beautiful," he said softly, sliding a fingertip along the neckline of her bodice. "But I'll tear it off of you if you don't take it off *now*."

She nodded, her eyes wide. Her hands shook as she began to unlace the dress. He watched, his eyes dark as the front parted. Then her hands shook too much so he reached up to take over. Strong fingers made short work of the lacings, but instead of pushing it off her shoulders, he held the dress together as he looked down at her.

"You're safe with me, Hope," he promised. "I'll never hurt you. We'll go slow. I promise."

"I know you won't hurt me. I trust you," she whispered, looking up at him as she lifted her hands to push at his. The dress slid off her shoulders, whispering down over her figure to pool on the floor.

She shivered, naked before him. For a moment, the taunts of her stepfamily came back to haunt her. That she was too small, too skinny... that no one could ever want her or love her.

Taking a deep breath, she locked her knees and

looked up. Only to find him looking down at her with a stunned expression.

"You are... *fuck,*" he cursed, reaching out a big hand but pausing halfway as though he was scared to touch her. "I'm a monster. I don't—" He sighed, running his hand through his hair. The look he shot her was tortured. "The things I want... you're way too good for me."

"Don't you dare!" she hissed, stepping closer and pressing herself boldly against him. "Kiss me. Kiss me again. Now."

He groaned as she lifted onto her toes, rubbing herself against him as she pressed her lips to him. Then the dam broke. And not just broke but exploded and shattered beyond repair.

He tumbled her backward onto the bed, bracing himself on his forearm as he pulled her beneath him. His lips crashed down onto hers as a hard knee pressed between her legs, parting them so he could settle between them. She gasped, clinging to his muscled upper arms as he slid his free hand down her body to explore her curves.

His hands were large and warm, coarse with calluses that told the story of a rough life. His lips moved over hers, alternating teasing her to get her to respond and then growling as he took over and controlled the kiss. Taking what he wanted... what they both wanted.

She gasped, arching her back to press her breasts against the broad solidity of his chest as his hand slid between her thighs. He slid his tongue against hers at the same time he stroked his fingers between her pussy lips.

She gasped, her hips rocking as he discovered how slick and wet she was. He growled in approval as he smoothed the evidence of her arousal up and over her clit. Sparks exploded behind her eyes and she moaned, the sound lost under his lips.

He still had his pants on, and the feeling of the fabric against the inside of her thighs made her shiver again.

"You're still dressed," she complained, running her hands down his body until she found his waistband. She fumbled with the ties, desperate to feel him against her, but couldn't figure them out.

With a grunt he moved his hand to tear them open and then went right back to touching her and teasing her clit with circles and strokes.

She moaned in pleasure against his lips and slid her hand into his pants. His cock, caught by a fold of the tight fabric, burst free and filled her hand. Butterflies rioted in her stomach. He was *huge,* bigger than she'd thought. Maybe they wouldn't even fit...

"Touch me," he broke the kiss to order roughly, his hand closing over hers on his erection and making her stroke him. Rougher and harder than she would have.

He groaned, watching her as she touched him. She found a thick bead of precum leaking from the tip. "Harder. Make me wet for you," he murmured, teasing her lips with his as she did as he ordered.

He touched her again, each stroke making her shiver and bringing her higher and higher. The tension in her lower body wound so tightly she thought she'd shatter from it.

Then he slid a finger deep into her body, and she gave a little cry, her back arching at the new sensation. "Gods, you're so tiny and tight. We should go slow…"

"Fuck slow!" She dug her nails into his shoulder, stroking him harder. Faster. She couldn't get her fingers all the way around him. "I'm not a virgin. We can totally do this."

He reared back for a moment, searching her expression. Then he seemed to reach a decision and pulled his hand away. Before she had chance to miss his touch, he was back. Covering her hand with his, he moved and pressed the broad head of his cock against the entrance to her body.

Her breath caught as he pushed in, stretching her body around him.

"You're mine, Hope," he murmured, capturing her hands again and pinning them above her head. "I… *mine!*"

She couldn't answer as he pushed harder, sliding halfway into her in one, solid push. It should never have been possible, but it was. Biting her lip, she watched him watching her. He pulled back and thrust again. Two more hard thrusts and he was buried all the way inside her. She bit her lip. She'd never felt so full in all her life. Not that she had *that* much experience, but it had never been like this before.

He kept his hips motionless, throbbing within her, and leaned down to claim her lips in a soft, gentle kiss.

With a small moan in the back of her throat, she kissed him back, their lips clinging.

The kiss didn't stay soft for long. His lips grew harder and more dominant. He moved his grip on her wrists to one hand, keeping her pinned down as he pulled back again. She whimpered as he pulled out, feeling every inch as he withdrew. He filled her again in one hard, fast thrust, setting up a brutal pace that rocked the bed beneath them.

She moaned, moving with him. The power and control in every line of his body thrilled and aroused her. She lifted her legs, wrapping them around his lean hips.

"*Fuck!*"

He swore as the changed position slid him even deeper within her and dropped his head as if to catch his breath. Or retain control.

Letting go of her hands, he wrapped his arms around her. He slid his arm under her shoulders, arching her up off the bed and cradling the back of her neck in his big hand. She almost pouted as she missed the soft scrape of his talons against her skin. She liked the elven look on him, but it was too smooth, too polished. She preferred his natural look.

With her hands released, she was free to touch him, and she did. Sliding her hands up his arms, she reveled in the feel of the hard muscles covered in satin skin. Now that she'd started, she couldn't stop touching him.

He sped up, his thrusts getting harder and faster. She wrapped herself around him, the tension in her body matching his. Nothing mattered apart from moving with him, her world narrowing down to just the two of them, his lips on hers... the next thrust as he buried himself inside her.

Her breathing caught as between one breath and the next she was there. Heat and need hit her broadside, her body aching as she clenched around him. He drove in one more time, rocking against her, and that was it.

She shattered apart with a scream, transported to heaven as he sped up. Three thrusts later, he slammed home and threw his head back to announce his climax with a roar that rattled the stones of the walls around them.

~

*H*ope was... like no female he'd ever been with before.

The next morning Graal lay on his back with his little human "wife" tucked up against his side, gently stroking her hair as the early morning sun streamed through the window. The servants had already been in and left them breakfast, careful not to look toward the bed where he and Hope lay entwined. He didn't care what they saw of him. He'd parade naked around the court, if necessary, but he didn't want anyone seeing Hope when she was vulnerable.

They'd come and gone. He could smell the food and coffee laid out for them, but he couldn't bring himself to move. It was too warm and comfortable here in the bed with Hope wrapped around him. Plus, he was, in a word, exhausted. He'd spent most of the night taking her in every way possible until, with a soft laugh and a hand on his chest, she'd begged him to let her sleep.

He had—never let it be said he wasn't a considerate lover—but only after he'd taken her gently one more time. She was like a drug, and he just couldn't get enough of her. The only thing that would make things perfect would be taking her under the moonlight after he'd chased and pinned her in the traditional orcish claiming chase. Such a chase would bind her to him for the rest of their lives.

He shivered and closed his eyes, imagining it as clear as day. He wanted that, wanted to claim Hope as his own, but... even though all his orcish instincts said to just do it and make it happen, he knew he couldn't.

Hope had to make that choice herself, just as Kelly had made the choice to come back to Karak. It wouldn't work otherwise. Now, after getting to know Hope, his conversations with Kelly made a lot more sense. Humans were not orcs, but they weren't weak-willed or stupid. They were strong and courageous. Hope had proven that every day—from facing down the witch to navigating the faery court.

He just had to hope that, when given the option, she would choose *him.*

Slight movement next to him made him look down to the sight of his beautiful little bed partner waking up. And she was adorable with it. She sighed softly, curling up like a cat against him and wrinkling her nose.

"Hey..." he said softly, making her eyes open slowly. For a moment they were unfocused and sleepy, but then she smiled, and it was like the sun coming out from behind the clouds.

"Hey, Monster," she murmured, her voice hoarse from sleep and the amount of screaming she'd done last night. "It can't be morning already," she grumbled, snuggling in against him. "Just five more minutes."

"It's still early," he told her, pulling her closer with a sigh of contentment. "We have plenty of time."

She gave a little sound somewhere between a rumble of approval and a kittenish purr. It was adorable, and he wanted to hear more little chirrups like that. Like say... every morning when he woke with her in his arms.

"Do we have to go to the tournament today?" she murmured sleepily. She wriggled until she could look up at him, using his arm as a pillow. "Can't we just stay in bed instead?"

Oh hell yeah, he'd love that. He dropped a kiss on the mussed curls at the top of her head. "Mandatory attendance, sweet thing. Queen's orders. All knights, male and female, have to participate."

She wrinkled her nose. "Even that asshole champion from last night. What was his name again?"

"Uh-huh, even him. Naebalar." He wasn't worried about the great lord champion. He could beat the guy with one hand tied behind his back, but that would reveal he was far more than the elf he was pretending to be.

"His wife seemed nice," she commented. "Poor woman, having to live with him."

He frowned, staring up at the ceiling as he recalled the conversation he'd had with her last night. Hope lifted up on one elbow, looking at him with a frown.

"What is it?"

"She spoke to me last night."

"Who? Naebalar's wife?" Hope frowned. "What did she want?"

He moved, pillowing his head with his arm to look at her. "She said I looked like my father."

"Huh, really? Did she know your... wait, wasn't your father an orc?"

He nodded. "There are very few females of my kind, and we know all those born to them."

God did they know all those with orc mothers, like Vekk. The asshole never let them forget his mom was Ione the Invincible, one of the most feared orc warrioresses in their history.

"So if your dad was an orc... how does an elf know him?"

He waited, watching her put two and two together in that clever little brain of hers. Her eyes widened, and she let out a small gasp. "She's... no, she's not your... is she?"

"My mother. Apparently."

"Oh shit." She sat up next to him. "And she recognized you? Do you think she'll tell her husband? We have to get out of here!"

He chuckled as she threw herself in front of him, looking at the door as though she expected the champion and all the queen's forces to come barreling through it at any moment. The fact that she thought to protect *him* warmed his heart. She was such a tiny, fierce little thing. She'd make a wonderful mother, fiercely protective of her kids.

An image of her holding a tiny orc baby with his eyes and her dark hair filled his mind, and he sucked a breath in. He wanted that, he *really* wanted that.

"I don't think she'll hand me over to the authorities," he said as he pulled her back into his arms. "I think she just wanted to talk. Now, are you ready for some breakfast?"

CHAPTER THIRTEEN

"Good morning, my lords, ladies, and gentlemen!"

The queen's voice rang out over the tournament field and those assembled there. The outer walls of the castle had expanded again, like they had last night, to bring the enchanted wood into the ballroom. Now a tournament field lay adjacent to the main courtyard.

The queen stood before her throne, set up on a dais beneath a canopy to shield her and her ladies of the court from the harsh glare of the sun. "I am pleased to see so many of you with us, especially after last night's celebrations."

Polite laughter rippled through the crowd, but Graal kept his snort to himself. No one would dare not be here this morning. Queen Oonais was known to consider nonparticipants in her events as traitors, and no one wanted to join Gudvar chained by his neck and wrists to the stone post in front of her.

"And," she continued over the laughter, motioning in irritation to indicate she hadn't finished, "I have an extra special surprise for you today!"

Graal had to suppress the urge to roll his eyes. The queen loved dramatics but even so Gudvar—an orc in the middle of the fae court—was impossible to miss. He heard whispers among the crowd, and someone had already thrown a tomato at Gudvar, the remains of which were still splattered across his massive chest and one shoulder.

"Thanks to the diligent efforts of my heroic champion, Lord Naebalar," the queen announced, a sweeping hand indicating the small dais, which was a miniature replica of her own set to the right of the canopy, where Naebalar sat. He smiled and acknowledged the attention from the crowd like a little princeling.

The champion was alone on his dais. Just one seat sat on the raised platform with no evidence of his wife. Graal's eyes narrowed as he looked for Lady Adharian, finding her toward the back of the crowd of ladies beneath the queen's canopy.

Once again, the Lady of Sharnwood was not with her husband and seemed to be actively avoiding notice. Her husband preened like a puffed-up peacock, behaving as though he were single and unencumbered. Yet Graal knew that he and Lady Adharian had been married for many years, since just after his birth. It was a drop in the ocean of an elf's long lifetime but not long enough for such contempt to have formed. He'd even seen Naebalar leaving with a couple of giggling young women last night. His lip wanted to curl in disgust. Many fae nobles had affairs, but to carry on in such a manner in front of everyone and shame his wife... and they called his kind cruel.

Unless... his mother had said their union was not her choice. Had she still been in love with his father all these years? Or had her husband somehow found out that she'd borne a half-orc babe?

Such a stigma lay around carrying an orc's get that if a woman were known to have carried such a child, she was usually ostracized by her family and community. Which meant most women bore such babies in secret, leaving them in the woods to be found. Like he was.

The queen watched the champion preening, smiling at him indulgently. Rumors had it the champion had eyes on the queen's bed, and beyond that, a place at her side. Graal didn't think Oonais was that stupid, though, to not see through the small-minded lord's machinations.

"Thanks to Lord Naebalar," she said. "We have the orc threat right *here* in this very court!"

The crowd gasped as she indicated the big orc in front of her, as though they'd only just noticed him. Like anyone could miss a nearly seven-foot behemoth like Gudvar.

"As a special treat, I am proud and pleased to announce that the winner of the tournament today will have the immense and unique honor of executing this foul creature right here on this very field!"

Graal froze as applause burst out around him,

trying not to let his gaze slide to where Gudvar was chained. He could easily win today's tournament, but he couldn't afford to. It would jeopardize their mission for the witch. If it were just him, he'd say fuck it, free Gudvar right now, and they could cut their way through the fae court in a bloody swath toward freedom. But he couldn't risk it. He couldn't risk Hope's life.

Also, if he won the tournament, he would be expected to kill Gudvar, and that simply wasn't happening. Gudvar had always hated his guts for reasons Graal had never worked out. But they were orckin, and no way would he ever hurt one of his own or allow one to come to harm.

However... his thoughts circled... He couldn't allow anyone *else* to win the competition and kill Gudvar instead, not while he could do something about it.

Fuck, fuck, fuck. He was screwed either way.

Graal sighed as he leaned down to fasten his greaves. This was utter bullshit, a fancy show with bling and braid boasting a murder as a finale, all tied up with a neat bow.

The court's knights were all in attendance, showing off in their shiniest armor. It was nothing like the training sessions in the orc camp where armor and mail was serviceable and functional rather than polished to a blinding sheen and no fucking braid was in evidence.

The whole thing was little more than an ego-trip for those involved—a way to show off in front of the queen and the ladies of the court. He looked up to where the women sat under the shade of parasols.

Hope was at the side of the tent, her delicate skin protected by the canopy above her. The witch's spell had dressed her in a pretty pink gown today, and his thoughts shifted. He couldn't wait for the lunchtime break to peel it from her in the small tent that had been allocated to him for the tournament.

Fully attired for the fight ahead, he walked toward the ladies' dais. He clinked and clanked all the way, which irritated him. How the hell did they *move* in all this shit?

He wasn't the only knight headed toward the ladies of the court to beg them for a favor to carry into battle. Since he had no argument with any of them—other than the fact they were elves and if he'd met them on the field of battle, he'd have cleaved their heads from their shoulders with his war sword without a second thought—he automatically course-corrected to avoid bumping into anyone as he made his way toward Hope.

Even if they hadn't been posing as a married couple, she would still have been the only female present who held any interest for him. He still couldn't believe what a lucky bastard he was that she'd given herself to him. *She'd be giving herself to him again at lunch and all night tonight...*

Just the thought sent a bolt of heat to his loins, and he almost missed the knight approaching from his right. His instincts warned him at the last moment, a shiver making his hackles rise, and he turned just as Lord Naebalar was about to bowl him over.

Instantly realizing that he couldn't get out of the way completely, he stopped trying, half turning and setting his weight so the elven warrior literally bounced off him. The witch's spell could conceal a lot, making him look a lot leaner and less muscled than he actually was, but it couldn't reduce his actual mass. Which meant the champion bounced off him, landing on his ass in the dirt right in front of the ladies' tent. His fancy blackened armor got dirty before they'd even started the day's games.

The crowd went silent, tension rolling through the air as Naebalar leaped to his feet, his cheeks flaming scarlet. "How *dare* you, sir! I demand satisfaction!"

Graal blinked. "I think, sir, that your argument is with Mother Earth for daring to besmirch your attire."

"You threw me to the ground," the elf snarled.

"I am but a simple knight from Faeranthorn," Graal replied mildly. "How could I hope to beat the best knight of the court, the queen's champion no less?"

The lord's eyes narrowed. Graal was saying all the right things, and he knew it. It would be hard to take offense for what was, in actuality, his own fault.

The queen certainly seemed to think so, standing and clapping her hands as she called out.

"Gentlemen, gentlemen... save it for the tournament field, please. My ladies and I look forward to the entertainment! Now, my knights, if you wish to claim a favor, please do so!"

Graal nodded sharply to the champion. "My lord."

Then turning, he made his way directly to where Hope sat. She was on the edge of her seat, concern in her dark eyes. It warmed his heart to see her worried about him, even though she had no reason to be. He could twist that little prick up in knots without breaking a sweat if he was in his real form. Hell, if he was in his real form, they'd all flee in panic anyway. The might of the fae army was in their numbers. One on one they were no match for an orc.

But... it boded well that she was concerned for him. A female should be concerned for her male's welfare. He was her protection, and she was his comfort. He knelt before her, his head bowed in a chivalrous gesture.

"My lady, would you do me the honor of allowing me to carry your favor into battle."

For a moment she looked blank, and he smiled, reaching for her hand. His finger hooked under the ribbons at her cuff, and he pulled gently. "It would give me great pleasure to wear these to win a victory today for you."

"Oh." Her lips formed a soft "o" of realization. "Yes, yes, of course!"

Pulling her hand free, she untied the ribbons. Her hand on his shoulder, she stood and reached up to plait them into the long fall of his hair.

For a moment, as she touched him, everything else... the tournament, their quest at the court, rescuing Gudvar... all fell away as he savored her nearness to him. A delicate scent rose from her skin.

He'd stood this close before, but now he knew what she felt like beneath him. What the sensual embrace of her tiny body felt like around his cock...

And he couldn't wait to feel it again. Lunch couldn't

come quickly enough because he already knew what was on his menu...

~

Contrary to Graal's earlier impression, the tournament was in fact, hard fought. The knights might have been wearing their best armor, but that didn't mean they were lacking in either effort or skill. Every category was a harder battle than he'd expected, and he was forced several times to reassess his impressions of elves as individual fighters.

Always before he'd discounted them when they were on their own since a single elf was no threat to an orc. It was a simple matter of facts. Orcs were bigger, stronger, and faster than their elven counterparts. They always ran in groups for that reason, and a *group* of the little bastards was definitely a threat.

But now, he was beginning to see that some of them were better trained than he'd thought. Even though he was having to moderate his strength and speed to avoid giving himself away, several times one of his opponents surprised him. Especially a lady knight with hair like midnight whose armor said plainly she was from the Black Plains.

But after lunch, things really got serious. The younger knights had been knocked out of the running for the tournament prize, so the bouts got harder. Graal grabbed a drink of water after his last bout ended, suppressing his anger as he looked over to the queen's dais.

Gudvar knelt in front of it, chained by his hands and neck to a stone post. Sensing someone's eyes on him, he looked up, flicking black hair matted with blood back as he looked around. Spotting Graal, he stared at him for a second and then looked away and spat on the ground in disgust.

Relief rolled through him at the playacting. Gudvar had recognized him. There was no question of that. If Lady Adharian was telling the truth and he looked *that* much like Braestak, his father's battle partner would certainly see through the enchantment. If anyone realized they knew each other, they were both fucked. And not in a fun way.

The sound of clapping brought his head around, and he turned to see the queen on her feet in front of her throne.

"Ladies and gentlemen of the court. The scores are in and we have our final two competitors!" she announced, waving her hand. A scroll appeared in the air in front of her. "And they are..."

The court held its breath as they waited for her to make the announcement.

"Lord Naebalar, my own champion and... Lord Larreth of Faeranthorn!"

Graal frowned and straightened up to his full height at the queen's announcement. That couldn't be right. No way could he be in the final two. He'd been careful to conceal his strength and ability so no one would figure out what he was. He'd made sure to lose a couple of bouts, unlike Naebalar, whose bouts he'd been watching when he wasn't fighting. The champion was a bully, using intimidation to make his opponents yield.

Knowing others were watching him, he'd been careful in his out bouts, making sure not to show his entire skillset. He knew he needed to keep a few aces up his sleeve for his final bout. He hadn't expected it to be against the champion, though.

But now he didn't bother to hide the confidence and self-awareness in his movements as he walked toward the central arena where the final bout would take place.

Lord Naebalar was already in the middle of the arena. He turned with a swirl of his purple-lined cape, looking Graal up and down.

"This will not take long," he scoffed to the cohort surrounding him. "I'll have this country bumpkin on his ass and crying for his mother within minutes."

Graal chuckled, the sound low and dirty as he loosened his sword in its sheath. "You might not want to talk about mother, my lord. I hear yours is fond of riding orc cock."

The insult had the predictable result. Naebalar went purple.

"You knave! I *will* have satisfaction for such vile lies!" he spat.

Graal shrugged. "Satisfaction is what she was looking for from what I hear, and your father's flaccid cock just wasn't enough."

As an insult, it was fairly mild, but either Naebalar wasn't used to the psychological aspects of such combat or Graal really had hit a sore spot about his mother. He screamed and launched himself at Graal, his sword raised to slash wildly.

Someone screamed as he leaped back, arms spread to avoid his guts spilling onto the ground. Naebalar swung again, but this time Graal was ready for him. Snatching his blade from its scabbard in one swift movement, he blocked the champion's swing. Then the fight was on in earnest.

Naebalar was a good swordsman, one of the best in the fae court, but Graal was an orc. He'd been fighting since he was born—first to stay alive and then in the orc camps. Training as an orc warrior started young and was brutal. Some of them didn't survive childhood. A *lot* didn't survive their first couple of battles. But he was neither young nor inexperienced anymore. His scars, hidden by the enchantment, were testament to his skill and reputation on the battlefield. And he brought all of that to bear with Naebalar.

They danced around each other, Graal turning all of the champion's attacks with ease. The clash of sword steel filled the air as Naebalar grew steadily more frustrated. Graal was taller and broader with a greater reach, so the champion couldn't physically best him. And, he had to admit, Naebalar was good. Fast and agile, he tried to whittle away at Graal's defenses, looking for an opening.

Graal grinned to himself. The fae wouldn't find one. Orcs weren't pack attackers. They were used to fighting alone against multiple opponents. So just one was child's play.

They locked sword hilts, the elf snarling right in

Graal's face. "You are not worthy to be on the field with me," he hissed. "When I've killed you, perhaps I'll pay your pretty little wife a visit."

Graal saw red. No one threatened Hope, not ever. With a snarl, he slapped Naebalar's blade aside with more brute force than skill.

"Keep her name out of your fucking mouth," he growled. "Don't even fucking *think* about her."

Pivoting, he slammed three hard blows against his opponent's sword, each one heavy enough to rattle Naebalar's skeleton in his skin. Shock showed on the champion's face as Graal beat him back, step by step, toward the edge of the arena. He couldn't kill the asshole. That would mean certain death for him and Hope, but to win the fight, he didn't have to. All he had to do was force Naebalar out of the arena.

So he picked the asshole up and threw him out. The champion bounced on his ass in the dirt, kicking up billows of dirt and dust.

The crowd roared as Graal turned, punching the air in victory. He'd won. He'd won the fucking stupid tournament and emerged the victor. He exchanged a look with Gudvar, who inclined his head a fraction of an inch in grudging respect. It was the nearest thing to acceptance the older orc had ever given him and meant more to Graal than winning a hundred fae tournaments.

He turned again, reveling in the exaltation of the crowd. He'd won. He was the champion—

"Graal!" Hope screamed. "Behind you!"

CHAPTER FOURTEEN

ime slowed for Hope. She held her breath as
Graal spun in what seemed like slow motion
but could only have been a couple of seconds. His silver
hair spun around his broad shoulders. The champion
was right behind him, rising like a wraith with a blade
in his fist. Her heart lurched as Graal brought up his
arm to block the blow intended for his throat.

He heard a collective gasp from the crowd as he
knocked the blade aside, a thin line of scarlet welling
over his forearm.

"Foul!" A female knight leaped to her feet, shouting
from the sidelines. "Larreth had won! Naebalar's attack
was illegal!"

"Wait!" The queen frowned, standing as Graal
turned ashen and dropped to one knee, his chest
heaving as though he couldn't draw breath.

"Graal!"

Hope raced down the dais steps, crossing the space

to her fallen lover in a heartbeat. She dropped to her knees in the dirt at his side.

"What's wrong? Talk to me. Tell me what's wrong," she begged as she smoothed his hair back from his face, noting the wideness of his eyes and the ashen tinge to his face.

He gasped, his lips turning blue as he rolled over, collapsing onto his back.

"What did you do to him?" she screamed up at the champion, standing over them with a triumphant look on his face.

"He's been poisoned."

Hope turned to find the champion's wife kneeling in the dirt next to her, uncaring of the fineness of her gown. She tilted Graal's chin up, drawing a symbol on the front of his throat with gentle fingers. It flared gold for a second, and he managed to gulp in a ragged breath.

"Thank you," she whispered, relief flooding through her as Graal sucked in air, getting oxygen to the rest of his body. She held on to his hand tightly as she glared up at Naebalar. If looks could kill, the elven champion would have already breathed his last.

"Why would you do that? Why poison someone because you lost? I thought knights were supposed to have honor!"

"Indeed," the queen said, her expression and tone unimpressed. "Lord Larreth beat you fairly, Lord Naebalar. Kindly explain yourself."

The champion grinned evilly and drew a symbol in

the air with the dagger anointed in Graal's blood. It was similar to the one his wife had used, but this one pulsed slickly in the air, like a poisoned heartbeat. Hope felt sick just looking at it as it faded away.

The mark on the front of Graal's throat disappeared, and he began to gasp for air again, his hand closing around Hope's. Pulling her closer, he looked into her eyes, and she saw resignation of his impending death in his.

To her utter horror, his skin began to change as well, the natural green color reasserting itself as the witch's enchantment began to dissolve.

The crowds of the court gasped as Naebalar bowed to the queen. "Because, Your Majesty, I had my suspicions about 'Lord Larreth.' I've spent a lot of time in Faeranthorn, and I have never once heard of a Lord Larreth. As soon as I saw him on the tournament field, I knew he had never been trained as a fae knight... his martial technique does not have the skill or grace of ours. And if he's not fae then, there's only one thing he can be..."

"An orc," the queen whispered, her eyes wide as she looked down at the fallen man at her feet. "He's an orc."

"A dying orc," Naebalar gloated. "The poison in his system will kill him within minutes."

"*No!*" Hope screamed, her hands on Graal's chest as fear and panic surged through her. "That's murder. You have to help him!"

She turned to the champion's wife. "Please, *do* something!"

The silver-haired elf had tears in her eyes as she shook her head. "I'm sorry. I can't."

"But you're his *mother*," Hope hissed. "You can't let him die!"

"I can't help him," Adharian answered in a tortured whisper. "I don't have the skill."

"Mother?" the champion sneered. "You fucking whore! I knew I never should have married you!"

Tears streamed down Hope's face as she clung to Graal. "Please! Someone has to help him!"

She couldn't let him die. She couldn't lose him. Not now. Not like this.

Trumpets rang out in a fanfare, and everyone looked up, even Hope. The air sparkled above the tournament arena, and between one breath and the next, a fairy appeared, her wings shimmering in the afternoon sun.

She looked at Hope.

"You're the only one who can help him, daughter of Howl."

"What? Me? How?"

Hope was reduced to single word replies as she looked up at the... fairy godmother? She certainly fit the bill with the wings and the flowing gown. All she needed now was the tiara and the wand.

The fairy floated down, her wings beating lazily in the air until she landed on her feet gently. A smile on her face, she reached down and touched Hope's cheek gently.

"You haven't figured it out yet, my dear? You are

Howl's Hope, the daughter he always wanted but needed to cross worlds to have."

"My father... was from here?" She blinked in surprise, but Graal's hand closing spasmodically around hers brought her back to what was important. "How does that help me now? *Save* him!"

"I can't," the fairy said firmly, "but you can. You have a foot in both worlds. Both human magic and sorcery run through your veins in equal measure. *Use* that."

"But how?"

"How else?" The fairy godmother spread her hands. "Why, True Love's Kiss, of course."

"True Love's Kiss? What are you on about?"

She looked sideways to Graal's mother for confirmation, only to find the elven woman and the entire court around them frozen into place. Even Graal was frozen, which also meant he wasn't suffocating still.

"True Love's Kiss," the fairy repeated. "It cures most things, even a curse or poison. All you have to do is kiss him."

She blinked. "That's it? Just a kiss."

"Ahh... no, my dear." The fairy crouched down, getting down on her level. Her beautiful face was serious. Deadly serious. "True Love's Kiss is not just any kiss. It's the most powerful magic there is. If you do this, you have to be sure. You have to love him... it *has* to be True Love. If not, the poison will accelerate and kill him. So, the question is... do you really love him. Is this true love?"

Hope parted her lips to answer, but no words emerged.

"If you don't," the fairy continued, "you can go home. Right now, to the life you should have had..."

A frown creased Hope's brow and she looked up at the fairy. "What do you mean?"

For answer, the fairy spread her hands and an image appeared in the air in front of Hope. Her mom's bakery in the sage green and pastel pink colors it had been originally, the ones Harold had painted over as soon as she'd died. Instead of her stepfather and brothers behind the counter, though... it was her. Older, with a few silvers in her hair, but undeniably her. The sign behind the counter read "Hope's Cafe."

"I look... happy," she whispered.

The fairy inclined her head. "A successful business, happy marriage, kids at college. You could have it all. You just need to say the word."

As she watched, the front door to the cafe opened, and a man walked in. Movie star handsome with a charming smile, he walked right up to future-her and kissed her passionately.

Not everything that is pretty is good, pumpkin... and not everything that is ugly means you harm.

The second part of her father's saying came back to her, and she looked at Graal. *Really* looked at him on the ground. The witch's glamour had disappeared, and he was back to his true, rough orc appearance.

And... she didn't care. She didn't care that he had green skin and tusks, that his skin was marked and scarred from his hard life as a warrior.

"I can't lose him," she whispered, the truth of her

words hitting her even as she uttered them. "I love him."

Ignoring the image of the possible future in front of her, she leaned down and pressed her lips gently to Graal's.

For a moment nothing happened, and her very soul cried. No, it had to work. She kissed harder, moving her lips against his unresponsive ones. Then, just as her heart was about to break, he shuddered and took a deep breath.

In the next instant, his arms were around her and he kissed her back, thoroughly and full of feeling. After a long moment, she pulled back to look down at him. His yellow-green eyes shone as he lifted a big hand, sliding it into her hair.

"You chose me," he whispered in a low rumble. "You could have had it all. That human... a life. And you chose me. Did you mean it? Do you... do you *love* me?"

The vulnerability in his eyes tore at her heart. He'd been let down and rejected in his life, abandoned as a baby. She could understand why he had trouble accepting she'd picked him.

"Yes," she said simply.

"It's my massive cock. I knew it," he announced, a twinkle of amusement in his eyes.

"Yeah, right. Of course it was," she agreed, slapping his shoulder. "And the fact you are the best man I know. You've kept me safe, been a gentleman... taught me to dance. And—"

He tightened his grip and pulled her down for

another kiss. "Hope, I did all those things because I love you too. I've loved you since the moment I saw you."

His kiss was slow and heartfelt, brimming with promise for the future. He pulled back and looked into her eyes. "I will love you to the day I die, my little human mate. This I swear."

The fairy cleared her throat and indicated the frozen crowd around them. "If that's all cleared up, I suggest I get you out of here. I can't hold this enchantment forever. Much as I'd like to keep Oonais locked like that for a good while."

The fairy grinned, and suddenly Hope recognized her.

"You!" She gasped. It was the witch. Younger, and prettier but undeniably her. "You... why did you send us here? Do you still want the apple?"

The fairy shook her head. "No, my dear. The quest was never about the apple. It was about *you*. I needed you to see the magic in your soul."

Hope looked at her askance, a hand in Graal's as he pulled her to her feet. "But... how? I thought humans don't have magic."

The fairy godmother shook her head. "It's not that humans don't have magic. It's that magic doesn't *work* on them. Not unless they want it to."

"What?" That didn't make sense. "But... the... you used a spell on us. On me?"

"Because you believed I could. And now you believe in *you*," she said gently, tapping gently on the center of her chest. "In here. And that's all I needed. Now, ready to go home?"

"No... wait, where are you sending us?" Hope checked but it was too late. The fairy waved the wand she hadn't had until right now, and the world disappeared around Hope and Graal in a poof of smoke and magic.

CHAPTER FIFTEEN

"I thought you said orcs couldn't sing?" Hope whispered as they made their way through the orc camp and passed a large green-grey orc crooning away as he plucked at what looked like the bastard lovechild of a guitar and a crocodile.

It was late at night and she had to rely on Graal leading her. Human night sight was nowhere near as good as an orc's.

Graal looked offended as he swept her up to cradle her against his broad chest. "*That* is not singing! One day I will sing for you, and you will be even more enraptured with me and want to ride my cock even more."

She arched her eyebrow. Since the witch had dropped them back at the orc camp earlier today, there had been scant little cock-riding. Most of their time had been taken up with questions and Graal reporting into his superiors about the fairy court and Gudvar. And Hope.

Her father had turned out to be some kind of hero in this world. All of the orcs she'd met regarded her with awe that she was Gunther Howl's daughter—all apart from the king's sorcerer Skali. Skali Howl, apparently her brother. Half-brother, anyway. She put their one, rather unpleasant, interaction out of her mind. She'd had her fill of asshole brothers, half or step. Graal was her family now, along with his friend Karak and his human mate Kelly. They'd also been reunited with Claw, with much tail wagging and cuddles.

"I *can* walk, you know," she protested at just being plucked off her feet but didn't wriggle to get free. Instead, she nestled closer, kissing along the side of his neck.

He growled as they left the confines of the camp. "Carry on like that, and this chase will be very, very short."

She nipped his earlobe playfully. "That's not the point of it though. Is it? You're supposed to chase and claim me."

"Oh... I will." His eyes flashed as he strode deeper into the forest that surrounded the camp. "And when I catch you, you'll scream my name to the night sky."

Pausing at the edge of a clearing, he slid her down the front of his body. The skirt of her thin white shift, the fabric so thin it was virtually transparent, ruched up around her thighs. But that was a minor thought as she registered the thickness of his cock pressing against her belly.

"Now," he rumbled when she was on her feet. "Run..."

And with a squeal of delight, she did.

~

"Are you sure you want to do this?" Graal asked, lifting a big hand to tuck a loose strand of her hair behind her ear.

Hope took a deep breath. They were back in the human world, a new enchantment in place to conceal Graal's orcish origins. Her mom's bakery was across the road, and she could just see Harold and his two sons inside. She didn't think of them as her family anymore.

And they had her stuff. Her mom's stuff.

"Yes. I want to do this. I *need* to do this." She nodded firmly and started across the road.

The bell on the door jangled as she pushed it open and stormed in like a galleon in full sail. Harold, at the counter, turned at the presence of a new customer, anger washing across his face as he spotted Hope.

"*You!*" he hissed. "How dare you show your face back here. Do you have any idea how much money I wasted on you, you ungrateful little bitch?"

"What? The money you stole from my mother?" she threw back, folding her arms. "The money you stole from my inheritance?"

"There was no money," Harold growled, advancing on her with violence in his eyes.

Before he could get anywhere near her, Graal stepped forward, putting his hands on her shoulders.

Harold stopped like he'd slammed into a glass door, his eyes widening. The spell this time hadn't slimmed

Graal down any. Instead, he was still just as huge and muscled as before. Dangerously huge and muscled. A low growl rumbled against her back from his broad chest, and she reached a hand up, squeezing his in warning.

"I want my things," she declared firmly. "And my mom's stuff. Now."

"Or what?" Harold sneered. "You'll get your handsome prince here to—"

She didn't let him finish, stepping up into his personal space. "I don't need anyone to fight my battles for me, Harold," she said, her voice icy. "Especially not against a small-minded bully like you. I'm not a weak child anymore, or an ill woman. Now get the hell out of my way before you find out how much like my *father* I really am."

He paled, his gaze shooting to Graal as something like realization filled his eyes. Standing aside quickly, he ushered his sons out of the way. They both looked surprised and started to argue.

"No!" Harold hissed. "Let her take what she wants and leave. Then we won't see her again."

She inclined her head. "Thank you, and no, you won't. I have a new life now."

Sweeping past him, she walked to her "room" to find her makeshift bed with its thin mattress was already gone. She ignored that and headed right for the storage boxes with the belongings she had and the few things she'd managed to save of her mom's.

"Let me take that," Graal rumbled, lifting it from her hands.

"Is this it?" he asked, looking around the dingy room. She could see the growing anger in the backs of his eyes as she nodded, wanting to get him out of here as quickly as possible.

"Yeah. Everything else was sold," she admitted sadly. She had nothing of her father's, not even his fairytale book.

He nodded, striding from the room. Harold and his sons watched them from the illusion of safety behind the counter. And she knew it was just an illusion. Graal could bat the whole thing aside without so much as breaking a sweat.

He paused as he reached it, turning his head to look them up and down. "You'll never see Hope again," he rumbled, his voice full of orcish growl. "But if you do what you did to Hope and her mom again, you'll definitely see me and my brothers."

Harold took a step backward, and even Hope could smell the fear leaching from his pores.

She reached out a hand and put it on Graal's.

"Come on." She smiled. "Let's go home."

umans. What was with this new obsession with humans?

Skali Howl, the king's sorcerer glowered to himself as he stared into the fire in front of him. He was slumped elegantly in a chair before it, his tent behind him. It was one of the finest in the camp, rivaling even Dread King Batak's.

Ever since Karak's human had come tumbling through the mists, whispers had been going around the orc camp. Humans, long since disappeared from the realms, had begun to reappear thanks to the mists. Most were just interested in them for bedsport. The orc race had precious few females and most were... not appealing. Certainly not as appealing to most as the weak little humans.

His lip curled back as he took a swallow from his wine goblet. They were pathetic delicate little things, weak of stature and lacking magic. He refused to believe the one brought back by Graal was his half-sister. No way had the mighty Gunther Howl produced something like *that*.

But he had to admit, his teeth grinding as he stared at the flames, at least the humans didn't look on them with fear like most of the populace in the lands the army moved through, always trying to reach or defend a front line that moved thanks to that fucking enchanted wood.

I knew about the queen and fairytales from my father's book.

He thought about that sentence, uttered by the human. His father's spell book, considered lost for nearly a century, was one of the most powerful artifacts of the realms. His father had been from a long line of warrior-sorcerers, his ancestors reputed to be the creators of the mist portals, and all their knowledge was distilled into that book.

He *had* to get that book.

Shoving to his feet, he dropped his goblet by the fire and turned to duck into his tent.

He was Skali Howl... the mists *would* obey him. He'd go to the human world and find his father's book.

Then he would use it to destroy the fae threat forever.

Thank you so much for reading Graal and Hope's story!
I hope you enjoyed reading it!

Want to find out what happened in that tent at lunch?
Get the FREE bonus scene when you sign up for my
newsletter at **minacarter.com!!**

The next book in the Mist-Rift Monster Romance series
will be Skali's story! Check my website for more details
on a release date!

PERFECT MATE

A hospital manager with a heart of gold. A soldier with a dark secret.

Lillian's life is... dull. The highlights of her day, other than her skinny hot chocolate, are the hunky guards who work in the military wing. It's classified and way above her pay grade, but she can't help feeling sorry for the hollow-eyed men and women they shuffle past reception. Then a late night emergency is wheeled in, his abdomen shredded and covered in blood. They're not an emergency room but she can't turn him away and risk a death on her hands.

Unable to get the handsome soldier out of her mind, Lillian sneaks into the restricted area and finds herself thrust into a world where nothing makes sense. A world where men aren't always men, the dead walk, and her handsome soldier is way more than he seems...

Her scent calls to him. She's his. Now he has to keep her alive.

Jack Harper was a soldier, a good one... then the Project decided to play god. Now he has permanent anger management issues and a monster living inside him. Used as a weapon, he's been waiting for a chance to strike back. But the Project are onto him.

Ruled unstable, a kill order is passed down on Jack and his squad and they are transferred to St.Margarets. Play-things for the head docs until a bullet to the back of the head deals with them for good. But Jack isn't going down that easily, not when the delicate scent he'd been waiting for all his life wraps around him.

The delicate human woman is his mate. And he'll fight anything the Project throws at him to save her.

Head on over to https://minacarter.com/book/perfect-mate/ to find out more!

ABOUT THE AUTHOR

Mina Carter is a *New York Times & USA Today* bestselling author of romance in many genres. She lives in the UK with her husband, daughter, a tank of a Staffordshire Bull Terrier and a bossy cat.

Connect with Mina online at:
minacarter.com

Join my VIP reader list and be the first to hear the news on book releases, AND be eligible for subscribers only bonus content, giveaways, special offers and free reads!

Don't miss out, sign up now!

SIGN UP HERE

facebook.com/minacarterauthor

twitter.com/minacarter

instagram.com/minacarter77

bookbub.com/profile/mina-carter

www.ingramcontent.com/pod-product-compliance
Lightning Source LLC
Chambersburg PA
CBHW061257120726
48001CB00001B/346